JOAN ELLIOTT PICKART

presents the powerful romance of a Plain Jane single mom burdened by a fourteen-year-old secret and the devastatingly handsome M.D. who makes her want to believe all things are possible—even second chances at love!

Praise for Joan Elliott Pickart

"Joan Elliott Pickart delivers an old-fashioned romance complete with appealing characters and...passion."
—*Romantic Times*

"Joan Elliott Pickart leaves you breathless with anticipation."
—*Rendezvous*

"[Joan Elliott Pickart] makes love magical, special, real, natural and oh, so right!"
—*Rendezvous*

"Joan Elliott Pickart weaves a sensitive love story...."
—*Romantic Times*

Dear Reader,

Welcome to Silhouette Desire! This month we've created a brand-new lineup of passionate, powerful and provocative love stories just for you.

Begin your reading enjoyment with *Ride the Thunder* by Lindsay McKenna, the September MAN OF THE MONTH and the second book in this beloved author's cross-line series, MORGAN'S MERCENARIES: ULTIMATE RESCUE. An amnesiac husband recovers his memory and returns to his wife and child in *The Secret Baby Bond* by Cindy Gerard, the ninth title in our compelling DYNASTIES: THE CONNELLYS continuity series.

Watch a feisty beauty fall for a wealthy lawman in *The Sheriff & the Amnesiac* by Ryanne Corey. Then meet the next generation of MacAllisters in *Plain Jane MacAllister* by Joan Elliott Pickart, the newest title in THE BABY BET: MACALLISTER'S GIFTS.

A night of passion leads to a marriage of convenience between a gutsy heiress and a macho rodeo cowboy in *Expecting Brand's Baby*, by debut Desire author Emilie Rose. And in Katherine Garbera's new title, *The Tycoon's Lady* falls off the stage into his arms at a bachelorette auction, as part of our popular BRIDAL BID theme promotion.

Savor all six of these sensational new romances from Silhouette Desire today.

Enjoy!

Joan Marlow Golan

Joan Marlow Golan
Senior Editor, Silhouette Desire

Joan Elliott Pickart

PLAIN JANE MACALLISTER

Published by Silhouette Books
America's Publisher of Contemporary Romance

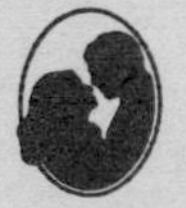

SILHOUETTE BOOKS

ISBN 0-373-76462-6

PLAIN JANE MACALLISTER

This edition published by arrangement with Harlequin Books S.A.

Visit Silhouette at www.eHarlequin.com

Printed in U.S.A.

Books by Joan Elliott Pickart

Silhouette Desire

**Angels and Elves* #961
Apache Dream Bride #999
†*Texas Moon* #1051
†*Texas Glory* #1088
Just My Joe #1202
Δ*Taming Tall, Dark Brandon* #1223
**Baby: MacAllister-Made* #1326
**Plain Jane MacAllister* #1462

Silhouette Books

**Her Secret Son*
◊*Party of Three*
◊*Crowned Hearts* 2001
"A Wish and a Prince"

Silhouette Special Edition

**Friends, Lovers...and Babies!* #1011
**The Father of Her Child* #1025
†*Texas Dawn* #1100
†*Texas Baby* #1141
Wife Most Wanted #1160
The Rancher and the Amnesiac Bride #1204
Δ*The Irresistible Mr. Sinclair* #1256
Δ*The Most Eligible M.D.* #1262
Man...Mercenary...Monarch #1303
**To a MacAllister Born* #1329
**Her Little Secret* #1377
Single with Twins #1405
◊*The Royal MacAllister* #1477

Previously published under the pseudonym Robin Elliott

Silhouette Desire

Call It Love #213
To Have It All #237
Picture of Love #261
Pennies in the Fountain #275
Dawn's Gift #303
Brooke's Chance #323
Betting Man #344
Silver Sands #362
Lost and Found #384
Out of the Cold #440
Sophie's Attic #725
Not Just Another Perfect Wife #818
Haven's Call #859

Silhouette Special Edition

Rancher's Heaven #909
Mother at Heart #968

Silhouette Intimate Moments

Gauntlet Run #206

*The Baby Bet
†Family Men
ΔThe Bachelor Bet
◊The Baby Bet: MacAllister's Gifts

JOAN ELLIOTT PICKART

is the author of over eighty-five novels. When she isn't writing, she enjoys reading, gardening and attending craft shows on the town square with her young daughter, Autumn. Joan also has three all-grown-up daughters and three fantastic grandchildren. Joan and Autumn live in a charming small town in the high pine country of Arizona.

For my grandsons,
Jeremiah, Frankie and Wolf,
The next generation

Prologue

Home, Mark Maxwell thought as he set his heavy suitcase down. He was finally back in Boston after living and working in Paris for what had proven to be a very long year.

The research project he'd been invited to take part in had been fascinating and challenging, and it had certainly been an honor to participate. The problem with his stay had been that the preconceived vision most Americans had about the city had turned out to be absolutely true. Everywhere he'd gone, it seemed, he had been surrounded by couples who were deeply in love.

Maybe the same could be said of Boston, but he'd sure never noticed it if it was. He'd gone to Paris with a mind-set which no doubt made him more aware of the love-in-bloom, or some such thing. To his own self-disgust, he'd also been thrown back in time to when he, too, had been in love, had lost his heart and youthful innocence to a sweet smile and sparkling brown eyes.

They had made plans for a future together, a forever, had talked for hours about the home they would share, the children they would create, the happiness that would be theirs until death parted them.

But none of it had been real...not to her.

She'd smashed his heart to smithereens, leaving him stunned, bitter and determined never to love again.

He'd been convinced that he'd dealt with those painful ghosts, had long since forgotten her and what she had done to him. But while in Paris in the crush of the clinging couples, the pairs, the twosomes, the old memories had risen to the fore, taunting him, making him face the realization that he really had neither forgiven nor forgotten her.

He strode across the living room toward the kitchen. While he'd been gone, he'd rented his apartment to his buddy Eric, a recently divorced doctor at the hospital, and Eric had told Mark on the phone the other night that he'd have some food in the refrigerator when Mark returned. He'd also put the magazines and junk mail that had come in Mark's absence in a box in the corner of the kitchen.

As Mark scrambled four eggs in a frying pan,

adding shredded cheese and chunks of ham, he inhaled the delicious aroma, then frowned as he scooped the mound of eggs onto a plate and carried it to the table at the end of the kitchen. He poured himself a glass of milk, then settled onto a chair and took a bite of the hot, very-needed food.

Yep, he thought, after a nourishing meal and hours of sleep, he'd be the same ol' Dr. Mark Maxwell who'd left Boston a year ago.

But he was still frowning as he stared into space as he chewed, then swallowed.

The same ol' Dr. Mark Maxwell, his mind echoed.

Dr. Mark Maxwell, who had avoided becoming involved in any kind of serious relationship with a woman for the past fourteen years.

Dr. Mark Maxwell, who had buried himself in his work, who was the whiz kid of medical research at only thirty-two-years-old.

Dr. Mark Maxwell, who was just as lonely here in Boston as he'd been in Paris, but who hadn't admitted that to himself until right this second.

"Damn it," he said aloud, then shoveled in another forkful of eggs. He was so thoroughly exhausted that he was emotionally and mentally vulnerable. He didn't seem to possess the ability to recognize that he had had no time to nurture a partnership with a woman because he'd been centered on his career.

His hopes and dreams had become a reality beyond his wildest imagination. But emotionally? He was forced to accept what he could no longer deny. He was still a kid, eighteen years old, wounded and raw, disillusioned, bitter and mad as hell.

"Well, isn't this just great?" Mark said, shaking his head in disgust. "So? Now what, Maxwell? How do you plan to free yourself of her ghost?"

He didn't have a clue. But, by damn, he'd figure it out once he'd had some rejuvenating sleep, because he had no intention of spending the rest of his life alone and lonely because of *her.* No way.

"I'll get back to myself on this later," he said, getting to his feet. "Damn straight, I will. But for now I'm not thinking about it anymore because I'm definitely brain-dead."

He went to the box in the corner, snatched up the magazine lying on the top of the pile and looked at the cover.

"Across the USA," he read, then sat down again and flipped it open.

Taking the last bite of eggs, Mark turned a page in the magazine and stiffened, every muscle in his body tensing as he stared at the story headline.

"Ventura, California, Cousins Marry Royal Cousins in Romantic Fairy-Tale Fashion," he read aloud.

His heart thundered as he looked at a color picture of a multitude of people whom the caption identified as being the two families...the royal one from the Island of Wilshire and the one from Ventura.

And there she was.

She was standing in the row behind the two recently married couples.

It was *her*.

Mark got to his feet so quickly, the chair fell to the floor with a crash he didn't even hear, his gaze riveted on the photograph.

This was creepy, really weird, he thought frantically. He was fighting an emotional battle over her and now her picture was staring him in the face?

Get a grip, he told himself, setting the fallen chair back into place and sinking onto it. Maybe this wasn't weird. Maybe this was a...yeah...a sign, a directive, telling him that the only way to be truly free of her was to see her one last time, making it possible finally to close the door on what had happened so very long ago. *Then* he'd be able to move forward, find his soul mate, fill his life with love and laughter, hearth, home and babies, and erase the chill of loneliness consuming him.

He'd sleep on this concept, he thought. But if it still had this much merit when he was well rested, he was going back to Ventura, by damn. He would fly to the opposite end of the States and get his heart back because somehow, *somehow,* she'd managed to keep it.

Mark picked up the magazine and stared at her picture, seeing the smile he knew so well, the blond hair and big, brown eyes, those lips...oh, those lips that tasted like sweet nectar.

She was so damn beautiful, he thought. She was

a mature woman now, not a child of seventeen. She'd gained weight over the years, but it suited her and...she was really, really beautiful and...

He smacked the magazine back onto the table and pointed a finger at her smiling image.

"You are going to have a visitor," he said, a rough edge to his voice. "It's payback time, Emily MacAllister."

One

"Grandma," Emily MacAllister called as she crossed the sunshine-filled kitchen. "I'm here with the flowers as promised, and they're gorgeous. You're going to love them. You can sit on the patio and supervise while I stick them in the ground. Grandma?"

"I'm in the living room, dear," Margaret MacAllister answered.

Emily went through the formal dining room and on to enter the living room, a smile of greeting for her beloved grandmother firmly in place.

Then she stopped dead in her tracks, feeling the color drain from her face and her breath catch as her heart thundered.

In that second, that tiny tick of time, as she stared

wide-eyed at the tall man who had risen to his feet when she appeared, her life as she knew it ceased to exist.

She wasn't thirty-one-years old, she was eighteen.

She wasn't a pudgy woman with fat cheeks and a hint of a double chin, she was a slender teenager with a figure to be envied.

She wasn't wearing clothes that looked as though she'd borrowed them from a bag lady, she was dressed in the latest designer jeans with a well-known brand name stitched across the pocket on her trim, tight bottom.

A wave of dizziness swept through Emily, and she gripped the top of an easy chair with one hand as the room spun around her.

This, she thought frantically, was not happening. It was a nightmare, and she was about to wake up and start her day in a normal manner.

Mark Maxwell was not, not, not, standing on the other side of that room, looking at her with no readable expression on his face. No.

"Isn't this a lovely surprise, Emily?" Margaret said pleasantly. "Mark is here to visit us after all these years."

No...he...isn't, Emily thought. Oh, why didn't the alarm go off and wake her up? No, no, no, Mark Maxwell is not here.

"Hello, Emily," Mark said quietly.

Yes, he is, she thought, pressing one hand to her forehead. But this wasn't skinny, gangly, endearingly geeky, Mark Maxwell. Nope, not this one. This Mark was at least six feet tall, had drop-dead-gorgeous rough-hewn features, broad shoulders and was wearing perfectly tailored dark slacks.

Where was the adorable plastic pocket protector jammed full of pens he always wore in his shirt pocket? Where was the cowlick in his light-brown hair that formed a cute little curlicue on the crown of his head? Where were the arms and legs and enormous feet, all of which were much too big for his still-developing body?

"Emily?" Margaret said. "Aren't you going to say hello to Mark? I realize that you two parted on, shall we say, terms that were at best confusing to the rest of us but, my stars, that was years ago. Old news. History, as the young people say. And you're not being very polite."

"Oh." Emily drew a much-needed breath, only then realizing she'd totally forgotten to breathe. "Sorry. Yes. Polite. Hello...Mark." She narrowed her eyes. "Why on earth are you here?"

"Emily, for heaven's sake," Margaret said. "That was extremely rude."

"That's all right, Margaret. I'm sure that my arriving unannounced like this is a bit of a shock to Emily."

Emily, Mark's mind hummed. There she was. He could hardly believe he was here with only a matter of feet separating them.

There was that silky blond hair he used to sift his

fingers through, now worn in gentle waves to just above her shoulders.

There were those classic MacAllister brown eyes that could sparkle with merriment, turn smoky with desire, shimmer with glistening tears when she was very happy or terribly sad.

She was dressed like a walking rummage sale, weighed a lot more than when she was a teenager, didn't appear to have on a speck of makeup and one toe was actually poking through a hole in her about-to-fall-apart tennis shoes.

Oh, yes, there she was.

Emily.

And she was absolutely beautiful.

He wanted to cross the room, pull her into his arms, kiss her senseless, then…

Hold it, Maxwell, Mark thought. This was Emily MacAllister, who had somehow managed to keep a stranglehold on his heart and he was there in Ventura, by damn, to get it back.

"Mark just returned from a year in Paris, Emily," Margaret said, "where he was part of a carefully selected team of medical researchers. His position in Boston was filled when he went to Paris but before he decides where to work next, perhaps even leaving Boston, he's taking a much-deserved vacation, which included stopping in Ventura to say hello. Isn't that nice?"

"Just too nice for words," Emily mumbled, then

inched around the chair and sank onto it as her trembling legs refused to hold her for another moment.

Mark sat back down on the sofa and propped one ankle on his other knee. Emily's gaze was riveted on the taut muscles visible beneath his slacks as he completed the masculine motion. She blinked and redirected her attention to the fingernails of one of her hands as though they were the most fascinating thing she'd ever seen.

"There are a couple of reasons that I stopped over in Ventura," Mark said. "One of them is to extend an apology to you and Robert, Margaret, for not keeping in better contact with you. Sending a Christmas card once a year just doesn't cut it.

"If you hadn't taken me in, welcomed me into your home when my father was killed in that accident when I was a senior in high school, there's no telling what grief I would have come to in the foster-care system. I owe you a great deal, and I feel as though I've been remiss in expressing my gratitude."

"We were delighted to have you here as a part of our family, Mark," Margaret said. "Even if we had had a crystal ball to tell us what would eventually transpire between you and..."

"Grandma," Emily interrupted, "let's not go traipsing down memory lane, shall we?" She looked at Mark. "You said you had a couple of reasons for being in Ventura?"

Mark nodded. Emily waited for him to continue speaking. One second, two, three...

"Is this a guessing game?" Emily finally said, frowning. "Do you intend to share this other... mission, with us?"

"All in good time," Mark said, then paused. "Margaret told me that you have a very challenging career, Emily, and that you've recently moved your business out of your home and into an office downtown.

"You research the history of old homes and buildings, as I understand it. Fascinating. Margaret also said you do quite a bit of work for the restoration division of MacAllister Architects so they can restore old structures in such a manner they will be eligible for registration with the historical society. Not only that but your reputation for excellence is spreading up and down the coast."

Emily glared at her grandmother. "Did you remember to tell him that I brush my teeth in the morning when I get up and again before I go to bed, Grandma?"

Margaret laughed. "Don't be silly. Mark asked how you were, what you were doing, and I told him. A proud grandmother has the right to boast. It's in our job description. We'd already moved on to the subject of the exciting events of Maggie and Alice's weddings and their new lives on the Island of Wilshire."

"Good topic," Emily said, pointing one finger in

the air. "There's nothing like a couple of royal weddings to put a little zing in the daily grind.

"Jessica is married now, too, Mark. She's a successful attorney, crazy in love with a police detective named Daniel, and became an instant mother to a darling baby girl named Tessa. We MacAllisters have spent a lot of time going to family weddings in..."

"But you've never married?" Mark interrupted quietly, looking directly at Emily.

"Me?" she said, splaying one hand on her chest. "Oh, heavens, no. When I was young and immature and such a starry-eyed child I thought I wanted that type of lifestyle but it suddenly dawned on me that it just wasn't my cup of tea and..."

She flipped one hand in the air. "Well, you know all that because you and I were inseparable from the time you moved to Ventura until you zoomed off to fame and fortune in Boston and... Well, silly us, we were so sure we were deeply in... We were so young and dumb, weren't we? Oh, my, yes. Well, that's enough of that subject."

It was enough of that subject, Mark thought, to slice and dice him, to hear spoken in Emily's own words an echo of what she'd written in that letter she'd sent him in Boston so many years ago.

His first instinct then had been to get on a plane and fly back to Ventura, confront Emily, make her look him right in the eye and repeat what was in that letter. But he hadn't had two nickels to rub together, let alone money for airfare. And besides, she'd made it perfectly clear in that damnable, hateful letter that it was over between them, so what was the point?

And now here he sat in the same room with her over a dozen years later hearing her say it all right to his face. And it still hurt. God, it hurt.

Well, wasn't this an efficient use of time? During the very first meeting with Emily since arriving this morning in Ventura, he'd gotten the cold, hard facts he needed to begin to retrieve his heart from her uncaring stranglehold.

But…

There was something just off the mark about what she had just said. She made it sound as though they'd mutually agreed that their feelings for each other weren't what they'd believed them to be, and that wasn't even remotely close to the truth.

He had left for Boston with the heartfelt promise to send for her just as soon as he could figure out a way to provide a home for her while he attended college on the scholarship he'd received.

Emily had vowed to wait for him no matter how long it took, but about a month later the shattering letter had come and…

"Yo in the house," a voice called in the distance, jerking Mark back to the present. "I'm here as ordered to dig in the dirt."

Emily's eyes widened and she jumped to her feet. "Can't. No digging in dirt today. Sorry, Grandma,

I've got a killer headache so we'll do this tomorrow. I'll just go tell… Bye, Mark, enjoy your vacation and…"

The front door of the house opened and an adolescent boy came into the living room.

"Oh, dear heaven," Emily whispered, "no."

"Hi," the boy said. "Didn't you hear me holler? I came right over on my bike when I got home from swimming and saw your note, Mom. Hi, Great-Grandma. We're going to dig the dirt, plant the plants, do it to it." His attention was caught by a tall man across the room getting slowly to his feet. "Oh, hi. Sorry. Didn't know there was company." He looked questioningly at his mother.

"Yes, well," Emily said, having difficulty breathing. "I…Mark Maxwell, I'd like you to meet…" She drew a shaky breath. "…my…my… son. Trevor. Trevor MacAllister. Trevor, say hello to Dr. Mark Maxwell. He's an old school…chum of mine."

"Cool," Trevor said, nodding. "Hi."

"You're Emily's…son?" Mark said, his voice sounding strange to his own ears as he stared at Trevor.

"Yep, that's me. Her genius-level offspring. Do note that I'm taller than she is already. Cool, huh?"

"Very cool," Mark said. "How…how old are you, Trevor?"

No! Don't answer that, Emily thought, taking a step toward Trevor.

"Yes, the time has come for this," Margaret whispered to no one.

"I'm twelve, almost thirteen," Trevor said. "Closer to thirteen, so just go with that. I'm about to become a bona fide teenager."

Who looked *exactly* as he had at that age, Mark thought, his mind racing. Tall, lanky, feet like gunboats, arms and legs seeming too big for his yet-to-fully-develop body, brown eyes, light-brown hair and a cowlick creating a curl on the crown of his head.

This was Emily's son? Mark's mind screamed. Oh, he didn't doubt for a second that she had given birth to him but, by damn, this boy standing a room away from him was more than just Emily's son.

There was no doubt in his mind. None.

He, Mark Maxwell, was Trevor's father!

Two

Just after ten o'clock that night, Emily stood in front of the full-length mirror mounted on the back of her bedroom door and sighed as she stared at her reflection.

Blimpo, she thought dismally. The jeans and over-blouse she was wearing made her look like a Pillsbury Dough Girl, complete with pudgy cheeks.

Her hair was freshly shampooed and her light makeup was just enough to accentuate her signature MacAllister brown eyes, but nothing could erase the fact that she weighed twenty pounds more than she should.

She'd been so proud of herself, of the thirty

pounds she'd lost during the past months, but to-night the twenty extra she still carried around made her thighs, stomach and bottom look like heavy sandbags and her face like a moon waiting for a cow to jump over it.

"Blak," Emily said, then left the bedroom, smacking off the light as she went.

She wandered down the hall into the small living room, aware that the sound of Trevor's stereo had stilled and there was no light shining from beneath his door as she glanced along the hallway.

And now Mark would knock on the door, she thought, sinking onto the sofa. It didn't require magical powers or a crystal ball to know that he would appear on her doorstep as soon as he was assured that Trevor...that his son...was asleep for the night.

She'd seen the look on Mark's face when he'd stared at Trevor that afternoon and saw the carbon copy of himself when he was young and skinny.

A shiver coursed through Emily. She wrapped her hands around her elbows as she moved to the edge of the sofa cushion and bent over slightly.

She felt so strange, she thought. It was as though she was standing outside herself watching a drama unfold scene by scene, not knowing what would happen next.

The beginning of the story had starred a pretty, slender young girl and a not-quite-having-it-together teenage boy. They had been deeply in love and had created a child together, a baby boy who the hero knew nothing about.

Fast forward to the present for act two. The hero was now a successful and highly respected doctor in the world of medical research, and the heroine was a fat, unattractive woman, who was struggling to hang onto a modicum of self-esteem she had fought desperately to obtain.

As for the deeply in love part?

A portion of her heart would always belong to the Mark Maxwell who had left Ventura to follow his dreams.

The Mark who had been so serious, so determined to achieve his career goals so he could provide for her in the manner he was convinced she needed because she had come from a fairly wealthy family.

The Mark who wouldn't believe her when she said she didn't need a fancy home and oodles of *things,* that she just wanted to be his wife, for better, for worse, for richer or poorer.

Oh, yes, Emily mused, she'd never really stopped loving *that* Mark Maxwell, not completely.

But Dr. Mark Maxwell, who was now on stage in act two? She didn't even know how to talk to men like him…so handsome, well-built, confident and successful, able to have any woman who caught his fancy. A man who wouldn't give a chubby woman like her a second look.

Deeply in love? Oh, ha. The Mark who was going

to knock on her door at any second probably hated her with an intensity that was equal to the passion with which he had once loved her.

A soft knock sounded at the door and Emily jerked, tightening her hold on her arms.

"Mark read the script," she said, hearing the edge of hysteria in her voice. "Now comes the big scene, the ugly words and accusations and..."

The knock was repeated.

Emily closed her eyes for a moment, took a steadying breath, then got to her feet and went to the door, speaking as she opened it.

"Hello, Mark," she said, stepping back. "I've been expecting you."

"I'm sure you have," he said gruffly, coming into the house, then turning to look at her as she closed the door behind him. "I waited across the street until what I hoped was Trevor's bedroom light went out, then sat in my car another twenty minutes so he would definitely be asleep. My *son* is asleep, isn't he?"

Emily nodded, feeling suddenly exhausted, so weary it was difficult to cross the room and sink onto an easy chair. Mark sat on the end of the sofa and frowned as he stared at her. Several silent moments passed until the very air in the room was oppressive, making it difficult for Emily to catch her breath.

"One question," Mark said finally. "Just one

simple little question, Emily.'' He paused. ''Why? Why did you keep the fact that I have a son a secret from me? Why did you feel you had the right to do that?''

Because I loved you more than I loved myself, Emily thought wildly. Because I was so young and terrified when I discovered I was pregnant, needed you with me so much, but I was so afraid you'd give up your dreams to do the proper thing, marry me, help me with our baby, then come to hate me for destroying everything you'd worked so hard for and would never have because of me.

''I believed it was the best thing to do for everyone involved,'' she said quietly. ''What we had together was over and...''

''Oh, now wait a minute,'' Mark said, raising one hand. ''You pulled that routine at your grandmother's this afternoon. You made it sound as though we had mutually agreed to break things off between us. That isn't true and you know it, Emily.

''That's what your family has thought all these years, right? That we broke up before I left? That's what you told them so they wouldn't come charging after me in MacAllister fashion and bring me back here to marry you. Right?''

''Yes,'' she said, lifting her chin. ''My father was ready to drag you back kicking and screaming if he had to, but I told him...I told him that we didn't…we didn't love each other anymore, that what we had shared was over."

"You lied to them," Mark said, narrowing his eyes. "Why?"

"No, it wasn't a lie, not entirely. I wrote you the letter, Mark. I told you that since you had gone, I'd realized that I was much too young to really know what love was. The distance between us had made me come out of the clouds and face the fact that…that it was best to just end things between us and…

"So, okay, I told my parents that you felt the same way but…you can't possibly understand everything I was going through, Mark. You just can't."

I couldn't bear the thought of you eventually hating me, Mark, can't you see that? Emily's mind rushed on. You were all I had and I loved you so much. I felt so special and important, beautiful and loved when I was with you. To have you hate me? No, I couldn't stand the mere image of it in my mind.

I was never as self-assured as Jessica, didn't have her confidence, her ability to win friends simply by being herself. And I didn't have the courage to rebel, be a unique individual like Trip…Alice. I was just Emily, lost in the shuffle, always smiling, never making waves, just wanting to please everyone so I would be accepted and then? Oh, God, then there was you and you loved me. Me! I...

"If I hadn't come to Ventura now," Mark said, jolting Emily back to the moment at hand, "I'd have never known that I have a son, would I? Damn you, Emily MacAllister, you had no right to keep his existence a secret from me."

"I..."

"Well, guess what, lady," Mark went on, "the ball just came into my court. I fully intend to tell my son that I'm his father. I may have missed out on the first thirteen years of his life, but that is ending as of now."

Emily's eyes widened, and she felt the color drain from her face.

"Oh, Mark, please, you can't do this," she said, shaking her head. "You can't just suddenly announce that you're... It's too much for a twelve-year-old boy to handle, to deal with and Mark, Trevor believes that I loved his father, that he was a wonderful young man and we were going to get married, but then...he...was...he was killed in an automobile accident."

A strange buzzing noise roared in Mark's ears as though he'd suddenly stepped into the midst of a swarm of bees. He shook his head slightly to quiet the sound, only to hear the wild beating of his heart.

He was dead? he thought incredulously. Emily had simply erased him from this world with a few carefully chosen words? Yep, Trevor, your dad was a super guy but, hey, he croaked in a car wreck. Tough luck, kid, you're joining the rank and file of the multitudes being raised by a single mom because your daddy is dead, dead, dead.

My God, Mark thought, dragging both hands down his face, not only had Emily never felt about him as he had about her, she had been capable of wiping him off the face of the earth. Out of sight. Out of mind. Out of her heart where he had never really been.

"Incredible," Mark said, shaking his head. "Just when did you drop this bombshell on my son?"

Emily sighed. "Trevor has always had a great many father figures because of the size of the MacAllister family. It wasn't until he started school that he questioned why he only had uncles instead of having a daddy, too."

"So I died, so to speak," Mark said tightly, "when Trevor was about five years old."

"Yes. I informed everyone in the family that that was what I had told him and they agreed, although reluctantly, to go along with it. I also told them that I would never divulge your name to Trevor, would tell him just to envision a special angel in heaven whenever he wanted to think about his father. Trevor, I'm thankful to say, has never brought up the subject again."

"How convenient for you."

Mark ran one hand over the crown of his head. It was a gesture that was so familiar to Emily, so endearing, a telling sign that Mark was upset, stressed, and one that Trevor executed whenever he was emotionally disturbed about something.

"You never loved me at all, did you?" Mark said, narrowing his eyes. "Jessica was the homecoming queen, the cheerleader, the president of the student council and on and on. Trip was in her own little world of rebellion that set her apart from the ever-famous MacAllister triplets. You were caught in the middle, always trying to please everybody, attempting to...hell, I don't know...find your place, or space, or something.

"Then here I was, arriving in our junior year in high school. Poor funny-looking Mark Maxwell, whose mother had split when he was a little boy and who was being raised by an alcoholic father who finally wiped himself out by driving into a tree when he was drunk as a skunk.

"You found a purpose, a cause. You'd take pity on the weird new kid, be his girlfriend, which would give you a status you'd never had before. Plus you were romantically involved with a guy, which was great because neither Jessica nor Trip were going steady with anyone. And, hey, wow, you would even lose your virginity before your sisters did. Score points for Emily."

"Oh, Mark, don't, please," Emily said, feeling

the sting of unshed tears burning her eyes. "I *did* love you—as much as any seventeen-year-old can understand love. Don't make what we shared ugly, tacky, something to be ashamed of. It wasn't like that."

"No?" he said. "You sure were capable of turning that love off like a faucet after I left here. Then I was killed and became an angel five years later? Oh, yeah, that's really strong evidence that you loved me. What a joke. You used me, Emily, to feel special, to make it possible to have something your sisters didn't. You really outdid yourself, didn't you? I mean, hey, you even had a baby out of wedlock. Neither Jessica nor Trip would top that one."

"Don't," Emily whispered, tears filling her eyes. "Please."

"The truth bites, huh? Well, there's a lot more truth where that came from. Truth...I'm Trevor's father. Truth...I'm alive and well. Truth...I intend to tell my son exactly who I am."

Emily got to her feet and started across the room, stopping in the middle and pressing clutched hands against her stomach.

"Listen to me, please, Mark," she said, her voice trembling. "I know you hate me, but don't destroy my...our son because of your feelings toward me. I know I can't keep you away from Trevor, but won't you just be his friend, get to know him, let him get to know you? Then, when you've built a firm foundation with him, we'll find a way to tell him that... Oh, God, how do I tell my child that I lied to him?''

''Write him a damn letter,'' Mark said, getting to his feet.

''Mark, I'm begging you, please don't shatter Trevor's world. Don't do that to him. Think about *him,* what it will do to him if you just blurt out the truth. Can't you find it in your heart to take this slowly and...forget how you feel about me. Put Trevor first.'' Two tears slid down Emily's face. ''He's just a baby who needs to be treated gently, kindly, with love. Oh, Mark, please.''

Mark planted his hands on his hips and stared up at the ceiling for a long moment, before looking at Emily again.

''All right,'' he said. ''We'll do this your way...for now. For Trevor's sake. Make certain you understand that, Emily. I'm doing this for my son. I don't owe you a damn thing.''

Emily nodded jerkily.

''I'll be here to have dinner with you and Trevor tomorrow night.''

''What?'' she said.

''You heard me. You invited your old school chum, as you so quaintly put it, to share a meal with you and your son. There's nothing unusual about that. Trevor and I can talk, chat while we eat, which will break the ice. What time?''

''I...''

"What time, Emily?"

"Six o'clock," she said, her shoulders slumping. "We always have dinner at six."

"Fine. I'll be here," he said, then started toward the door.

"Do you still like sun tea with honey, instead of sugar?"

Mark spun around. "Don't go there, Emily. Don't even think of trying that routine. Don't attempt to soften me up with cute little trips down memory lane because it won't work and..." He paused and frowned. "Why did you remember a dumb detail like that, my liking honey in my sun tea instead of sugar?"

Because I loved you, you dolt, Emily thought. You don't like cloth napkins. You eat the seeds in watermelon because it's too much trouble to pick them out. Your favorite color is pale pink like the inside of a seashell, but you thought that sounded too girly so you always said it was blue. You like French fries but detest hash brown potatoes. These aren't dumb details, you idiot. They're memories. Mine. To keep...forever.

"Forget it," Mark said, continuing on to the door and opening it. "Good night, Emily. No, correct that. There hasn't been one good thing about this night. I'll see you at six tomorrow."

Mark closed the door behind him with a quiet click as he left, but even so, Emily cringed, feeling as though she'd suffered a physical blow. Two more tears slithered down her cheeks, and she dashed them away. She returned to the chair and sank onto it, staring at the door.

In the next instant she got to her feet and went into the kitchen where she opened the refrigerator freezer and reached for some comfort, some food, her shaking hand gripping a carton of ice cream. She snatched her fingers back as though they had been burned, and slammed the freezer closed with more force than was necessary.

Nearly running, she hurried to her bedroom, opened the top drawer of her dresser and picked up an exquisite mother-of-pearl hand mirror, which she hugged to her breasts as she settled onto the edge of the bed.

She closed her eyes and allowed herself to float back to the day in January when her grandfather had asked her to come to his study to receive the special gift he'd spoken of at Christmas. Each grandchild was to meet with Robert MacAllister privately and be given a present he'd selected just for them. Whether they told anyone what it was would be up to them.

Emily remembered, tracing one fingertip over the edge of the mirror that she had gasped in awe when she'd unwrapped the gift and seen the beautiful mirror.

It belonged to my mother, Robert MacAllister had

told her. *It always had a place of honor on her dressing table because my father had given it to her. Now? I want you to have it, Emily, for a very specific reason.*

Emily looked at her grandfather questioningly.

My mother taught me, Robert went on, *with that mirror, to see past the outer trappings of myself and understand, get to know who I was becoming within, to never lose track of the real Robert MacAllister.*

Emily nodded.

That's what I want you to do with the mirror, darling Emily. Gaze at your image in a private place when you're alone. Discover who you really are behind that smile you keep so firmly in place and beneath those extra pounds you've put on to put distance between you and the world around you.

Oh, Grandpa, Emily had said, her eyes filling with tears, *it's...it's safe being fat and unattractive and... I hide in here, just keep smiling as I've always done and say that I'm doing fine and...* She shook her head as tears choked off her words.

I know, Robert said gently. *You're also hiding in your house by running your business from there. It's time to step forward, Emily. The mirror will help give you the courage you need to accomplish what you must do. I love you, my sweet Emily. Come out of the shadows and walk in the sunshine.*

You're so wise, Grandpa. This is a wonderful gift

that I'll always cherish and I promise you that I'll try to do what you're asking of me. I will.

And she was, Emily thought, lifting the mirror so she could see her reflection. Right after the new year holidays, she'd gone to her Aunt Kara, who was a semi-retired physician, had a complete physical, then asked Kara to outline a healthy diet and regiment of exercise. Kara had agreed that Emily had fifty pounds to shed, a fact that Emily knew embarrassed her son when his fat mother was seen by his friends.

Slowly but surely the pounds had melted away, one after another. Thirty gone; twenty left to go.

''You still look like Porky Pig's sister,'' Emily said to her reflection. ''Mark must have been thoroughly disgusted when he saw how you've let yourself become a blimp.'' She paused and sighed. ''No, forget that. Mark doesn't give a rip about what I look like. He's too busy hating me because I...''

Emily got to her feet and replaced the mirror in the drawer.

There was no purpose to be served by tormenting herself with the long list of Mark's accusations. He believed that she had never loved him at all, which wasn't true. *It wasn't.*

She had never stopped loving the Mark Maxwell she had known when they were teenagers. She'd hidden in her cocoon of fat and inside her house, and when she became too lonely she'd reach within herself for that love, wrap it around her like a warm, fuzzy blanket as she relived the memories of what she'd shared with Mark.

But those days of hiding were over. She'd rented an office downtown two months ago and was a successful businesswoman who greeted the public with new confidence and self-worth.

And Trevor, her sweet, darling son, took his dessert to his room each night so Emily wouldn't have to watch him eat it while she wasn't having any of the calorie-laden treat. She was, indeed, stepping out of the gloomy shadows into the brilliant sunshine, just as her grandfather had wished her to do. If she didn't feel like smiling, by golly, she didn't smile.

Everything had been going so well, Emily thought, as she swept back the blankets on the bed. Until now. Until Mark had reappeared in her life and turned it upside down. An angry Mark. A handsome and self-assured Mark, who was so intimidating and made her feel fat and sloppy, vulnerable and…

It was as though, Emily mused, taking her nightie from beneath the pillow and starting toward the bathroom, Mark had somehow pricked her with an invisible pin, creating a tiny hole where the self-confidence and self-esteem that she'd struggled so terribly hard to achieve were slowly escaping, and she didn't know how to keep it from happening.

Emily stopped at the bedroom door, then went to

the dresser and took out the mirror again, staring at her frowning reflection.

"Get a grip, Emily MacAllister," she ordered herself.

She would *not,* she vowed, allow Mark to destroy the Emily she had become. No. She'd square her shoulders, lift her...darn it, her *double* chin, and decide *with* him how best to reveal his identity to her...their son.

There would be no more begging, pleading, acting like the child she had been when she had loved him. She didn't love him *now,* for heaven's sake, so her emotions, her heart, would not get in the way of making the proper decisions for Trevor.

No, she had no feelings whatsoever for the Mark Maxwell who had returned to Ventura after so many years.

None at all.

Did she?

Three

Honey instead of sugar in his sun tea.

"Damn it, Maxwell," Mark said to the dark room, "give it a rest."

He glanced at the clock on the nightstand next to the bed in his hotel suite and groaned as he saw it was after two o'clock in the morning. He hadn't even been able to doze since attempting to sleep hours before.

His mind, Mark thought angrily, was a jumbled maze of disturbing information he'd gathered while at Emily's house earlier that night.

"Yeah, Emily," he said, dragging both hands down his face, "I still like honey in my sun tea."

Even though he'd lashed out at her when she'd

asked him that, Mark thought, he'd known from the look on Emily's face and from the way she'd flinched when he'd yelled at her, that she hadn't been playing tricky games. Her asking him that question had been an honest reaction to her knowing he was coming to dinner.

And Emily had remembered after all these years that he liked honey in his sun tea.

And for reasons he couldn't begin to fathom, that fact warmed him to the very depths of his soul.

"Ah, I'm losing it," Mark said, dropping his arms heavily onto the bed.

He was on mental overload, that was for damn sure. He had nowhere to put all that he'd discovered since returning to Ventura less than twenty-four hours ago.

He had a son.

Trevor *MacAllister,* who from the moment he was born should have been Trevor *Maxwell.*

It was time, it was long overdue, for Trevor to know the truth.

Yeah, okay, he could see Emily's point that a news flash like that shouldn't be dropped like a bomb on a kid of that age. But the existence of Trevor, plus the package of lies that Emily had told her family wasn't all that was keeping him from getting the sleep he so desperately needed.

No, it was more than that.

It was Emily, herself.

Mark sighed.

Emily, his mind echoed. She was still so beautiful, so…her. In all his travels he'd never seen brown eyes as enchanting as Emily's. He'd never seen lips so perfectly shaped, so kissable. He'd never seen hands so delicate that they fluttered gracefully in the air like exquisite butterfly wings when she became animated. He'd never seen—

"You have three seconds to knock it off, Maxwell," Mark said aloud, anger and frustration making his voice gritty. "Or I'll strangle you with my bare hands."

Mark rolled onto his stomach, punched his pillow with far more force than necessary, then total exhaustion finally claimed him and he fell into a restless, dream-filled sleep.

"Why are you putting flowers in a vase on the table, Mom?" Trevor said. "I don't think you're supposed to do that when a guy comes to dinner. It's lame. Girl stuff, you know what I mean?"

"Company is company," Emily said, peering into the oven. "I'm simply setting an attractive table because we have a guest sharing our meal." She straightened and looked at Trevor. "You, sir, need to go take a shower and put on clean clothes before Mark gets here. Shoo. And shampoo your hair, too. If you don't get the chlorine from the pool out of it, it's going to turn green."

"Really? Cool."

"Trevor!"

"I'm going, I'm going," he said, stomping across the room. "Sure is a bunch of big deal about some old guy you used to go to school with. Geez. You'd think he was somebody important, for crying out loud."

As Trevor disappeared from view, Emily leaned back against the counter and sighed.

Important? Mark Maxwell? she thought. No way, Trevor. The man is only your father, who you believe is dead, an angel in heaven. The man who intends to inform you of his true identity in the very near future.

"Oh, what a mess," Emily said, pressing her fingertips to her temples as she felt a painful headache beginning to throb.

She glanced down at the pretty border print of bright flowers around the bottom of the white summer dress she wore, then smoothed the full skirt over what she knew were her much-too-broad hips.

She'd considered wearing a long-sleeved dress but that would have been uncomfortably warm for a July evening, she mused. So there she was in a square-cut neckline and no sleeves, chubby arms displayed for all to see. For Mark to see.

"So?" she said, pushing away from the counter. "There's just more of me to hug, that's all. Not that there's a long line of admirers panting to hug me but...oh, Emily, just put a cork in it."

She glanced at the clock on the kitchen wall and

saw at the same moment that the doorbell rang that it was exactly six o'clock.

Typical Mark, she thought, leaving the kitchen. He had a *thing* about being punctual. She'd learned to be ready to go when he arrived at her house to pick her up for a date because if she kept him sitting in the living room he got antsy and out of sorts.

He'd once stood in the rain on her front porch, getting soaked to the skin, because he thought it would be as rude to be early as it would to be late.

At the door, Emily hesitated, drew a steadying breath, then opened the door.

Oh, cripe, she thought dismally, Mark was just so gorgeous, so blatantly masculine.... Black slacks, a trendy gray shirt with no collar and— Why didn't he have a cowlick anymore? A person was born with a cowlick, and it was there for life. You couldn't just decide *not* to have a cowlick anymore, so...

"What happened to your cowlick?" Emily said, cocking her head slightly to one side.

In the next instant, as she realized she'd spoken her thought aloud, she felt a warm flush of embarrassment stain her cheeks.

"Never mind," she said quickly. "Come in, Mark. You're right on time, of course. I mean, you're...right...on time and— Oh, just come in."

Mark entered the house and chuckled as he moved past Emily. A funny little frisson of heat slithered down her spine as she heard the sexy, male sound. She gave the door a push and cringed as it slammed too loudly.

"You still blush a pretty pink," Mark said, turning to look at Emily. "I didn't think women our age did that. It's cute."

"That's me." Emily rolled her eyes heavenward. "Just-too-cute-for-words Emily. *Cute,* Mark, is not used to describe women who weigh what I do. However, I don't wish to supply you with adjectives that would apply, thank you very much."

"I think that you look lovely, Emily. I think that that's a very nice dress and that you're lovely."

"Thank..." Emily started, then completely forgot the rest of it as her gaze met Mark's.

She *was* lovely, Emily thought dreamily, and Mark was so ruggedly handsome and— Oh, my.

Emily was so beautiful, Mark's mind hummed. And she still blushed, causing her cheeks to glow like dewy peaches and...

The buzzer on the stove shrilled, and Emily jerked in surprise at the intrusive noise.

"Dinner is ready," she said, hearing the thread of breathlessness in her voice. "Have a seat on the sofa or something while I get it on the table.

"Trevor will be out in a second. He didn't think he needed to shower because he was swimming most of the day. I signed him up for the summer program at the community center so I'd know where he was while I'm working, and he's too old for a baby-sitter, but I wasn't about to just let him roam around on his own and...I'm babbling, aren't I?"

Mark nodded. "Just a tad. Yes."

"Well, I'm nervous, Mark," she said, throwing up her hands. "If you slip up and say the wrong thing to Trevor and he puts two and two together before we feel he's ready to know that you're..."

"I won't slip up," Mark interrupted quietly. "I don't intend to do anything to hurt him, Emily."

"Oh. Well, good. That's good." Emily started toward the kitchen. "Sit."

"Emily?"

She stopped and turned halfway to look back at Mark questioningly.

"In answer to your question regarding my cowlick," he said. "As I'm sure you've realized by now I was a late bloomer physically. I grew several inches and added pounds after I left Ventura. My hair became thicker, too, and the increased weight of it makes the cowlick lie flat. I believe that Trevor is going to be a late bloomer, too, from the looks of him."

Emily smiled and patted her ample hips. "I bloomed rather late myself, but I'm in the process of unblooming, or some such thing." She paused and frowned. "Why am I telling you this? I have no idea." She shook her head as she spun around and went on into the kitchen.

Mark sank onto the sofa and stared at the doorway Emily had disappeared through.

He'd felt it, he thought. The heat of desire that had coiled low in his body when he'd looked directly into Emily's enchanting brown eyes, familiar brown eyes, had been hot, burning with a bright flame of want and need.

He'd remembered in that moment that had lasted an eternity what it had been like to make love with Emily, with the woman he'd given his heart to for all time.

Damn. She could still turn him inside out and hang him out to dry. And she wasn't even trying to do it, he was convinced of that. She envisioned herself as fat and frumpy, or some such ridiculous thing, and sure wasn't attempting to seduce him so she could gain control of the situation.

No, Emily wasn't playing coy, womanly games. She was just being Emily. But what he'd better not forget, not even for one second, was that she had never really loved him, not as he had loved her.

Trevor entered the living room wearing baggy yellow shorts that came to the middle of his bony knees and an oversized brown T-shirt. His hair was beginning to dry and the cowlick was inching upward in a curl.

"Hey," Trevor said, slouching onto an easy chair.

"Hey," Mark said. "What's doin'?"

"Nothing." Trevor shrugged. "You?"

"Nothing," Mark said, with the exact same gesture. "I understand you like to swim."

"Yeah, and I'm good, too. I'm thinking of trying

out for the swim team at school in the fall. I'd have to keep up my grades, get all As and Bs to be on a sport team because that's the rule at school, but that's no sweat. Thing is, you know, I'm not sure I'd like a coach *telling* me to swim so many laps and junk, instead of just doing what I want to in the pool like I am now. Get the drift?"

"Makes sense," Mark said, nodding. "Maybe you could try out the theory and see how you feel about it."

"Like how?"

"Well, I'm just hanging out. I've rented an SUV. I could go to the pool with you, pretend I'm your coach and put you through some tough practice sessions. You'd know pretty quick if you liked to be barked at by a coach type."

"You'd do that for me?" Trevor asked, frowning slightly. "Why?"

Because you're my son, Trevor, Mark thought, drinking in the very sight of the boy. I'm your father, and I already love you in a special place in my heart that I didn't even know existed before now.

"Why not?" Mark said. "You game?"

"Game on," Trevor said, punching one fist in the air. "This is way cool." He paused. "But do you know, I mean *really* know about swimming stuff?"

"Yep," Mark said. "I was on the swim team at Ventura High back in the ice ages." Because when he swam he could blank his mind and not think about his drunken father. "Correct that. I was the *star* of the swim team. You can ask your mom about that.'' Emily was always in the bleachers cheering him on. Always. ''She'll probably remember.''

Emily appeared in the kitchen doorway. ''Dinner is on the table so...''

''Hey, Mom, guess what?'' Trevor said, jumping to his feet and nearly toppling over as the toe of one tennis shoe caught on the toe of the other. ''Mark is going to pretend he's my swim coach so I can...''

As Emily listened to Trevor's breathless and excited dissertation a chill swept through her. She wrapped her hands around her elbows. So, she thought, it's begun. Mark was already taking steps to get to know his son, to establish a rapport, a bond, with Trevor. This whole scenario was suddenly frightening her for reasons that weren't entirely clear in her jumbled mind.

Yes, she was worried about what Trevor's reaction would be to the bombshell they would be dropping on him. But there was more than that now, causing a fist of fear to tighten painfully in her stomach.

Was she so possessive of Trevor, so selfish, that she wanted him all to herself? Was she afraid that her son might prefer his father's company over hers?

Would Trevor realize that there would be no budget, no careful thought given to spending money of any great quantity if he lived with a doctor whose monthly paycheck was no doubt more than Emily made in six months? That could have great importance to an adolescent boy who wanted to dress in the newest fad clothes like his friends and have the latest videos and computer games. Once he was over the initial shock at their news, would Trevor announce that he wanted to go live with his dad?

Oh, Emily, stop it, she ordered herself. She was jumping much too far ahead, creating heartbreaking problems in her mind that were growing from her imagination, not from reality.

One step at a time here. The first thing on the agenda being that dinner was on the table and getting cold.

"That sounds great, Trevor," Emily said, managing to produce a small smile as Trevor stopped speaking and took a much-needed breath. "Now, let's eat before I have to rewarm everything I've already put on the table."

A short time later Trevor and Mark had filled their plates with crispy chicken, mashed potatoes and gravy, and ears of fresh, locally grown corn.

Mark glanced at Emily's plate and frowned as he saw one small piece of chicken, half an ear of corn and four slices of a peach. "That's all you're eating, Emily?"

"Mom's on a diet," Trevor said, then took a big bite of chicken. He chewed, swallowed and nodded in approval. "Good chick. Mom is doing super on her diet, Mark. She's not nearly as fat as she used to be."

"Thank you," Emily said, smiling. "I think."

"That's not a diet," Mark said, frowning as he looked at Emily's plate again. "That's starvation. You'll lower your energy level, Emily, and your resistance to illness and... Look at that. You took a bite of corn without even putting any butter and salt on it. Who invented this so-called diet of yours?"

"My Aunt Kara. The doctor? Remember?"

"Oh," Mark said, nodding. "Well, I guess it's okay then."

"Well, thank you ever so very much for your approval, Dr. Maxwell." Emily glared at him. "I mean, gracious, if you had any lingering doubts about my being sensible enough to do this properly, I'd just fill my plate with all those mashed potatoes and dig in. In other words, mind your own business."

"Wow." Trevor swiveled his head back and forth as he looked at his mother, Mark, then back to Emily. "You two must have been really good friends in school. I mean, you know, like you're still cool enough together to yell at each other and stuff."

"Yes," Mark said quietly, looking directly at Emily. "Your mother and I were very, very good friends back then. At least I *think* we were...friends."

"Yes, of course, we were." Emily averted her gaze from Mark's as a swirl of heat settled low in her body.

"Did you know my dad, Mark?" Trevor asked, reaching for another ear of corn.

The piece of corn Emily held fell with a thud back onto her plate as she felt the color drain from her face.

"Trevor," she said, aware that her voice was trembling, "we haven't discussed your father in years. Why are you asking Mark if he knew..." Her voice trailed off as she stared at her son.

"Just because you didn't want to talk about my dad," Trevor said, his voice rising, "and wouldn't even tell me his name, which is really stupid if you ask me, it doesn't mean I haven't thought about him.

"There's stuff I'd like to know, but the whole family just zips it if I bring up the subject. I'm not a little kid anymore, Mom. What are you protecting me from anyway? Was the guy a total sleaze, or something? Was this bit about my dad being a wonderful man a bunch of bull?"

"Easy, buddy," Mark said quietly. "Let's exhibit some respect here, huh? Yelling at your mother doesn't cut it, Trevor. Not in my book."

"Sorry," Trevor mumbled. "But, geez, I just want some answers and...hell, forget it."

"Watch your mouth," Mark said sternly.

"Yeah, okay," Trevor said, then sighed. "Sorry, Mom. I didn't mean to swear like that. I shouldn't have mentioned my father, either, because you get all sad when you talk about him, and so we don't talk about him, and I can go with that program. It's just that Mark is here, and you two were close friends and I figure he knows who you hung out with back then and... Never mind. What's for dessert?"

"Chocolate brownies," Emily said, her voice still unsteady. "I...I had no idea that you had questions about your father, Trevor. I thought it was a closed subject, that you were happy with the way things are. The two of us being a team, a..."

"Sure I am, Mom," Trevor said quickly. "I'm cool about this. Really. It's okay. Just forget I even brought it up. It was a dumb thing to do. Did you put frosting on the brownies?"

"Yes, I did, and chocolate sprinkles, too."

"Which means we'd better clean our plates," Mark said, "so we can dig into those brownies, Trevor. I, for one, am going to have another piece of that delicious chicken. How about you?"

"Sure," Trevor said, smiling.

As Trevor put another large piece of chicken on his plate, Mark looked at Emily.

"'The time has come, the Walrus said,'" Mark recited, "'to talk of many things.'"

"Yes," Emily whispered. "I guess it has."

"Huh?" Trevor said.

"Goggles," Mark said. "Do you have regulation swim goggles, Trevor?"

"No," he said, shaking his head.

"Well, as your new coach I insist you have a pair," Mark said. "How about I pick you up about nine tomorrow morning and we'll stop at the sporting goods store before we go to the pool and I'll buy you some? If, of course, all this meets with your mother's approval. Emily?"

"What? Oh, yes, it's fine," she said, nodding jerkily, "and extremely nice of you, Mark. What do you say to Mark, Trevor?"

"Oh," Trevor said. "Thank you."

"That's settled then," Mark said. "Emily, you've hardly touched your dinner, what there is of it."

"I..."

"She leaves half of it a lot of times. She said her stomach shrunk, or something, since she went on this diet big-time."

"I don't think Kara would be thrilled with that news," Mark said. "Eat, Emily, and don't tell me to mind my own business. You'll definitely pay the price if you don't have sufficient nourishment. I'd hate for that to take place because...because I care about what happens to you and... Just eat your puny dinner, would you?"

"I... Yes, I will," Emily said, meeting Mark's gaze. She picked up the ear of corn. "I'll clean my plate, but dessert is taboo."

"Fair enough," Mark said, smiling.

They continued to look directly into each other's eyes for an amount of time neither would have been able to say had ticked by.

Trevor shifted his own gaze back and forth between his mother and Mark, raising his eyebrows as he nodded.

"Cool," he said, smothering a burst of laughter with a forkful of potatoes.

Four

As dinner progressed, Mark asked for more details regarding the subject of Maggie and Alice MacAllister marrying into the royal family of the Island of Wilshire. Margaret had talked about it briefly the previous afternoon, he said, but she had been more interested in being brought up to date on his doings.

The island was a beautiful paradise, Emily told Mark, and the weddings had been like something out of a fairy tale. Trevor added his two cents by saying he was really glad he had got to stay put in Ventura with his best friend, Jacob, rather than go to weddings that were all gushy and mushy where everybody hugged and kissed and cried.

"Gushy and mushy?" Mark said, laughing. "I've

never heard weddings described quite like that before, Trevor. Plus there's hugging, kissing and crying, huh?''

''Majorly. I went to my Aunt Jessica's wedding when she got hitched to the cop. Daniel. He's my Uncle Daniel now and he is one very awesome guy. He's a detective and carries a gun, the whole bit. Anyway, I've never seen so much hugging, kissing and crying in my entire life.

''I finally ended up toting Uncle Daniel's kid around, that's baby Tessa, so nobody would grab me and kiss me or something. Weddings are the worst.'' Trevor glanced quickly at his mother, then Mark. ''Well, I guess it might depend on who was getting married. Know what I mean?''

''Not really,'' Emily said, then popped the last piece of peach into her mouth.

''Well, if *you* got married, Mom. I'd hug you and give you a kiss and junk, but don't count on me crying 'cause it isn't going to happen.''

Emily choked on the minuscule piece of peach and started to cough. Mark stood, reached across the table and whacked her on the back.

''Oh.'' Emily patted her chest. ''That's better. Thank you.''

''Take a sip of your sun tea,'' Mark said, sitting down again, ''with honey.''

''Mine is plain,'' Emily said absently, staring at Trevor. ''There are too many calories in honey. For the record, Trevor, I am *not* getting married. Ever.''

Why not? Mark thought.

"Why not?" Trevor said.

"Because…because I like my life exactly the way it is," Emily said, fiddling with the napkin spread across her lap. "It suits me just fine."

"Don't you ever get lonely?" Mark asked quietly.

"No," she said, meeting his gaze. Yes. But when she did she wrapped her memories of their time together around her like a warm, comforting blanket until the chill of loneliness eased. "I'm much too busy to get lonely."

"Give me a break," Mark said, with a snort of disbelief. "I often work eighteen-hour days, but I still have time to be lonely."

"You're lonely?" Emily and Trevor said in unison as they stared at Mark.

"Well, I…" Mark said, then stopped speaking and cleared his throat. "Yeah, okay, yeah, sometimes I… Hey, I'm just chatting here, going with the flow of the conversation, that's all."

"You need a wife, Mark," Trevor said decisively. "I never thought about whether grown-ups get lonely, but I guess they do sometimes. So, fix it." He slid a glance at his mother. "Find a nice lady, who can cook good and laughs a lot, isn't grumpy and stuff, then have a gushy, mushy wedding and you'd be all set. Right?"

"My, my, who is ready for chocolate brownies?" Emily said.

''It's not all that easy, Trevor,'' Mark said, totally ignoring the offer of dessert. ''A man and woman should be deeply in love, plus have trust, honesty, compromise, a whole list of things as a solid foundation supporting their relationship before they get married. That takes a great deal of heartfelt dedication and work.''

Mark shifted his gaze slowly to Emily and frowned. ''Some people just aren't cut out to take all that on. Haven't you found that to be true, Emily?''

''Chocolate brownies with chocolate frosting and chocolate sprinkles.'' Emily glared at Mark as she got to her feet. ''What is true, Dr. Maxwell, is that this is an insane topic to be discussing with a twelve-year-old boy who—''

''I'm almost thirteen.''

''Who,'' Emily repeated, ''won't even be entertaining the concept of falling in love, working at a relationship, then having a gushy, mushy wedding, for many years yet.''

She picked up her plate, marched to the counter, plunked it down, then spun around to face the table again.

''Therefore,'' she yelled, ''change the subject.''

Emily's eyes widened as she saw Mark's and Trevor's mouths drop open at the exact same moment due to her outburst, and then, in perfect synchronization, each of them swept a hand over the crown of his head.

She braced one hand on the counter and pressed the other against her forehead.

"I can't handle this," she mumbled.

"Whew," Mark said, shaking his head slightly. "You sure learned how to speak...holler...your mind in the dozen or so years since I've seen you, Emily. You used to just sort of smile and nod a lot."

"That was then, buster," Emily said, straightening and pointing one finger at him. "And this is now. I...am...woman." She burst into laughter. "Hear me roar!"

"Trust me, Mark," Trevor said, rolling his eyes heavenward. "My mom can roar with the best of 'em. You should hear her when I leave a wet bathing suit and towel on my bedroom floor."

Mark laughed in delight. "She cracks the plaster in the ceiling, huh?"

"Close, very close."

"All right, you two," Emily said, smiling as she brought the brownies to the table, "now you're ganging up on me. Do note that I haven't released my hold on this plate. These brownies can disappear before you get your paws on them, you know."

"Oh, sweet mommy," Trevor said, clasping his hands beneath his chin, "who never speaks above a whisper no matter how rotten I am, may I please have a chocolate brownie with chocolate frosting and chocolate sprinkles?"

"Will this get it done, Trevor?" Mark duplicated Trevor's pose. "At what point do we really beg?"

"Now is good," Trevor said, out of the corner of his mouth.

"Please, please, please," Mark and Trevor chanted.

"Here," Emily said, laughing as she shoved the plate at Mark who grabbed it with both hands. "You two are crazy, a real pair to draw to."

And she loved them both so much.

Emily snatched Mark's dinner plate from in front of him, picked up the now-empty platter that had held the chicken and went back to the counter.

She hadn't meant that the way it had suddenly popped into her head, Emily told herself frantically. Yes, of course, she loved her son more than life itself. But she did *not* love, was *not* in love, with the Mark Maxwell who was sitting there being fun and funny as he interacted with her…their…son.

It was the Mark of years before who she had loved, maybe still did, not that it mattered one way or another, because *this* Mark had nothing to do with *that* Mark, so—

"Great brownies, Mom," Trevor said, then reached for his second one.

"Very delicious," Mark said.

"Can I ride my bike over to Jacob's? I want to tell him about Mark acting like a swimming coach for me."

"*May* I ride my bike over to Jacob's," Emily automatically corrected.

"You don't have a bike," Trevor said, grinning. "Just kidding. Okay... *May* I?"

"After you clear the table, which is your job as you well know, and you head home the second the streetlights come on."

"'Kay." Trevor said, then took a big bite of brownie. "Mmm. Can...*may*...I take a brownie to Jacob?"

"If there are any left." Emily glanced over at the plate and the rapidly diminishing number of brownie squares remaining.

"I'll do your kitchen duty for you tonight, Trevor," Mark said.

"Cool. Thanks," the boy said, pushing back his chair. He took a clean napkin from the ceramic holder on the end of the table, wrapped up a brownie and stuck it in his shirt pocket. "I'm gone."

"I'll see you tomorrow morning at nine o'clock."

"I'll be ready." Trevor nodded. "Bye."

Trevor dashed out the back door and silence fell over the room. Emily rinsed the platter, put it in the dishwasher, then returned to the table for more dishes. As she reached for the bowl containing a small portion of potatoes, Mark caught her hand in one of his.

"That's my job this evening," he said, looking up at her. "Remember?"

What she remembered, Emily thought, unable to tear her gaze from Mark's, was the feel of this strong but gentle hand holding hers. What she remembered was the heat of desire pulsing low in her body that she hadn't experienced in many years. What she remembered was Mark when she had loved him so much it defied description in mere words.

"Guests," Emily said, then drew a needed breath as Mark continued to grasp her hand, "don't do kitchen chores in this house."

"I don't feel like a guest. This was a family dinner, and I took part in it. I haven't experienced anything like this since I lived with your grandparents after my father died. This evening was nice, very nice. I had a great time and you sure are a good cook. Thank you for...everything."

"You're welcome. You obviously got along famously with Trevor."

"It's a start. You've done a fantastic job of raising him, Emily. That is one terrific kid." Mark smiled. "One terrific *growing* boy who has an appetite like..."

"His father," Emily said. She left the dishes on the table, then tugged gently on her hand, which Mark didn't release.

Mark got to his feet, finally let go of Emily's hand and placed both of his on her shoulders, keeping a small distance between them.

"It really hit me tonight that I've missed out on so much of Trevor's life. I wish I had been here to see his first smile, first tooth, see him take his first wobbly steps, hear his first babbling baby words...

"Ah, hell, Emily, what happened? To us? To you

and the way you felt about me? We had so much together, and... I just don't understand. I've never understood how you could just stop loving me the way you did back then. Talk to me."

Emily shook her head. "There's no purpose to be served by rehashing all this, Mark. I was young, so immature, and when you left I just realized that.... No, I'm not going to do this. My family urged me to tell you that I was pregnant but..."

"Why didn't you?" he said, tightening his hands on her shoulders. "I would have come right back to Ventura. You wouldn't have had to go through all this alone. I would have wanted to be here with you, with our son."

And you would have given up all your dreams for a future in medicine, Emily thought. He'd have settled for some dead-end job to keep a roof over their heads and eventually...oh, yes, guaranteed...he would have hated her for destroying everything he had ever wanted, had worked so hard for. She'd loved him far too much to do that to him, and she would have died a little inside as she saw his love for her turn into resentment, then chilling hate.

"It would never have worked out," she said, staring at the center of his chest. "A baby isn't enough to sustain a marriage when one of the couple, one of the parents isn't...isn't in...love with the other. Mark, don't do this. Please."

"Look at me, Emily."

She slowly raised her head to meet Mark's gaze.

''The day I left for Boston you cried as though your heart was breaking because we were going to be separated. You told me over and over how much you loved me, would miss me, that you'd wait for me no matter how long it took until I could send for you.''

''Don't,'' Emily whispered, feeling threatening tears stinging her eyes.

''I remember,'' Mark went on, ''that when I kissed you for the last time your lips tasted salty from your tears, and it just ripped me up. For days, weeks, even months, I couldn't erase the memory of that taste, the tears I had caused you to cry.

''Even after I got your letter I still could taste those salty tears on your lips.'' He lowered his head slowly toward Emily's. ''Do you remember that kiss, Emily? Do you?''

''Yes, I do, but...'' Emily started, then stopped speaking as two tears slid down her cheeks, followed by two more.

''A kiss that tasted like salty tears,'' Mark said, his voice gritty with emotion. ''Just...like...this one.''

Mark's mouth captured Emily's, his tongue delving between her tear-moistened lips to seek and find her tongue. He pulled her close to his body, and her arms floated upward to encircle his neck as her lashes drifted down. He deepened the kiss even more, and Emily responded in total abandon, savoring every heated sensation that rushed throughout her like a raging river.

Just as when they'd first seen each other the day before in Margaret and Robert MacAllister's living room, Emily and Mark were flung back in time.

They were so young and so very much in love.

No one mattered, even existed, but the two of them.

They even talked, in lazy voices after making love, about sitting on a swing on their front porch and waving goodbye to their children and grandchildren after they'd come to visit.

They envisioned so many glorious scenarios of their life together, unfolding it reverently, like a map that revealed treasures to cherish for all time.

Mark broke the kiss to raise his head a fraction of an inch to draw a sharp breath, but before he could claim Emily's lips again, she landed back in reality with a jarring thud.

"No, Mark," she said, splaying her hands flat on his chest. "No."

Mark released his hold on her and she took a step backward, wrapping her hands around her elbows as she shook her head.

"You...we...shouldn't have done that," she said, then took a much-needed breath as she willed her heated body back under her control.

"Why not?" Mark said, frowning. "We just learned something, didn't we, Emily? We still want, desire, each other as much as we ever did. What do you think that means?"

"Nothing," she said, nearly yelling. "Nothing at all. Why? Because that kiss didn't take place in the here and now, Mark. That kiss took us back in time to when we were so young, so naive, so certain that everything we planned, fantasized and dreamed about was going to come true. We were immature children, not the adults we are now, standing here in this kitchen."

"The adults standing in this kitchen," he said, matching her volume, "shared that kiss, gave as much as we received. The desire burning in me isn't from fourteen years ago, Emily MacAllister. It's here, right now, and I dare you to deny that you don't desire me, too."

"The word *desire* belongs to our past, Mark Maxwell. Whatever sexual reaction our bodies had a few minutes ago was lust. Tacky lust, with no loving emotions involved."

"Do you really believe that?" he said so quietly that Emily could hardly hear him.

Yes. No. She didn't know, Emily thought frantically. She couldn't think straight. She was on fire with the want, the need, of Mark and... No, no, no, not *this* Mark.

"Emily?"

"Yes, I believe it. The past has to be kept separate and apart from the present. I truly did love you when I was that starry-eyed child, Mark. Please don't ever doubt that. I loved you as much as any girl stepping into the world of womanhood is capable of loving.

"But it wasn't deep enough, rich enough to last, because I was too young to understand the complexities of it all. I refuse to feel guilty for that, because we were both at fault, tried to have too much too soon."

She was piling lies upon lies, Emily thought miserably. She was diminishing what she had felt for Mark back then, and she hated what she was doing. But she had no choice.

There was no purpose to be served in telling Mark that she'd kept her pregnancy a secret from him so that he could achieve his dreams, his goals. No purpose whatsoever.

And so she had to lie and lie and lie, and the weight of those lies was crushing her.

"For heaven's sake, Mark," Emily said, throwing out her hands, "if you're still having a problem keeping the past separate from the present, then just stop and take a good look at me. What do you see? The slim, trim, size-six Emily whose waist was so tiny you could encircle it with your hands?

"Oh, ha. Reality check, Mark. I'm a very, *very* pudgy thirty-one-year-old woman, who gains weight by even smelling, or looking at something fattening. I have a twelve-year-old son, an ancient car that's held together with a hope and a prayer, a mortgage payment on this little house and a business that is growing steadily but is a long way from making me free of financial worries. Focus on those facts, not on what used to be."

"That's quite a list," he said, folding his arms over his chest.

"You bet it is."

"Except you left something out."

"Such as?"

"Feelings, emotions. Who is Emily MacAllister *now?* What makes you smile, laugh right out loud, or cry those salty tears of yours? What dreams do you have that replaced the ones you shared with me?"

"What difference does it make?" Emily asked, shaking her head.

"I don't know," Mark said, sounding suddenly weary. "You don't seem to be having any trouble keeping the past separate from the present, but it's not that easy for me, Emily. Maybe that's because I've been away and now that I'm back I'm slam-dunked with memories at every turn.

"Plus there's Trevor. Do you have any idea what it's like to discover you have a son you didn't even know existed? He's walking, talking, breathing evidence of what you and I had together back when.

"Emily, I came here to get final closure on us."

"Final...final closure?" Emily said, shock evident in her voice. "You've...hated me all these years?"

No, Mark thought, he'd *loved* her all these years. But now Mark narrowed his eyes because he knew she'd robbed him of Trevor's first smile, his wobbly steps, each tiny new tooth. He hadn't held Trevor's little hand to reassure him that everything would be fine as he took his son to school on that terrifying first day of kindergarten.

He hadn't taught him to throw a ball, or ride a bike, or how to tie his shoes.

He hadn't tucked him into bed at night, read him a story and heard his prayers.

He'd shared none of those things with his son because Emily had told Trevor that his father was dead.

And the pain of that truth was beginning to grow much bigger than that caused by her letter.

Anger was building within him, as well, Mark thought, steadily growing into white-hot fury and pushing aside the desire he'd felt for Emily when he'd kissed her. Getting his heart back from Emily MacAllister just might not be that difficult after all. She had made decisions she'd had no right to make. Played God. Set up her life the way she wanted it with no regard for his feelings, his right to know about the existence of his son.

His son. Who was going to be told that he, Mark Maxwell, was his father.

"You've called the shots for a dozen years, Emily," Mark said, "but now it's my turn. Yes, I agreed that it would be best for Trevor and me to establish a rapport before he's told the truth of who I am. But when I decide the time is right, I intend to sit him down and tell him who I am. When *I* decide the time is right."

"But..."

"And hear this, Emily," Mark went on. "I'll also inform my son that I didn't stay away because I didn't want anything to do with him. I'm going to tell Trevor that I didn't know he even existed until he walked into your grandmother's house yesterday. You'll have to deal with whatever ramifications there are when Trevor learns the truth. Lies have a way of catching up with people, Emily."

"Oh, Mark, wait. Please. We'll sit Trevor down together and talk to him, explain things to him, present a united front that will help cushion what he's being told, and—"

"You don't get it, do you?" Mark interrupted. "You're no longer pushing everyone's buttons, deciding how it's all going to happen. I'm back, Emily. You had a nice long run of controlling all of our lives, but it's over, finished, done. Oh, yeah, I'm back and I'm in charge now. Get used to it, because that's the way it's going to be."

Five

Emily's business, Then and Now, was housed in a small, one-room-plus-a-bathroom office in a strip mall. She had made it as homey as possible with numerous plants, two comfortable chairs fronting her desk and a low side cupboard with albums of photographs of projccts shc had taken part in. Against the back wall was a drafting table placed so she could see anyone who entered while she was working there.

In the middle of the afternoon following the dinner with Mark, Emily sat on the high stool in front of the drafting table and yawned. Then yawned again.

Oh, good grief, she thought, she was so tired.

She'd hardly slept last night as she'd relived every minute detail of the hours spent with Mark.

The man was driving her over the edge, she thought dismally. One minute he was kissing the socks off her and the next he was yelling in anger, declaring that he was in charge of things now, by golly.

Emily sighed and straightened on the stool, staring at the pen-and-ink drawing she was attempting to complete to be the cover for a contracted project. It consisted of an historical report on a turn-of-the-century house in Ventura, a copy of the inspection by the historical society and Emily's recommendations as to how those requirements could be accomplished.

She had been working for weeks on this assignment and had discovered a multitude of fascinating facts about the house and who had lived, loved and died there. All she had to do was finish this drawing, deliver the report and receive the much-needed check.

"So get to work," she ordered herself. "Draw your little heart out, Emily MacAllister, because your son is out-growing every article of clothing he owns...again."

Trevor, she thought. He was spending heaven only knew how much time today at the pool with Mark acting as his swimming coach. Were they getting along, becoming buddies, pals, a team of good ol' boys?

Would Trevor ask Mark again, since he had him alone, if Mark had known Trevor's father back in high school?

Dear heaven, she'd been so stunned when Trevor had broached the subject of his father at dinner last night. Had she been kidding herself all these years, playing ostrich, going merrily along believing that Trevor had no problem with his daddy-less status and the fact that she refused to reveal the identity of his father?

She had a sinking feeling in her stomach that that was exactly how it was. Trevor had kept silent on the subject for her sake. He'd changed the subject very quickly last night when he'd realized she was becoming upset, bless his heart.

Oh, Trevor, honey, Emily thought, closing her eyes. She'd done what she decided was the best for everyone involved, but mothers weren't perfect. At least not the mother named Emily MacAllister.

Her mind was a maze of worry and confusion. And her heart?

"Don't go there, Emily," she said, picking up the pen. "Just don't. Draw a window on this dumb house."

As Emily put the pen to paper the door to the office opened and she looked up, her breath catching as Mark entered. He shut the door and glanced around, before walking slowly toward her. Very slowly toward her.

Like a sleek panther stalking its prey, Emily

thought, swallowing a little bubble of hysteria. He moved with the easy, masculine grace of a man who was very comfortable in his own body. The Mark of old used to nearly fall on his head when he attempted to tie his shoes.

Mark stopped in front of the drafting table, glanced at the picture, then met Emily's wide-eyed gaze.

"Nice place," he said. "Professional but cozy." He paused. "The name you chose for your business is interesting, too. Then and Now. It sort of sums up where you and I are at the moment, too, doesn't it?"

"Was there something you wanted?" Emily said, aware that her voice was not quite steady.

You, Mark thought, then frowned. Damn it, where had that come from? He hadn't pondered over that answer, it had just been there the instant the question had been asked. And he couldn't deny the truth of his reply. He wanted, desired, wished to make love with Emily for hours, hold her, caress and kiss her, feel her tremble in his arms as her passion heightened.

But which Emily did he desire? The Emily of then? Or the Emily of now? Then and Now. How ironical that that was what she'd chosen to name her business.

"Mark?" Emily said.

"What? Oh, I stopped by to tell you that Trevor and I had a great time at the pool. I worked him hard and that kiddo will sleep good tonight, believe me. He's got the natural talent, Emily, could be a major player on the swim team and he's stoked about it, wants to try out for the team when school starts."

"Oh," Emily said, nodding. "Well, sure, that would be all right because he gets excellent grades." She smiled. "I can attend all the competitions that are held at Ventura High School. I think I wore a spot smooth on the bench where I always sat when I was cheering for you when you were the star of... Never mind."

"It meant a lot to me that you were always there. I swam for you as much as for me and the team."

Emily laughed softly. "Remember the state championship meet? I yelled so much I lost my voice for a week, but you guys won. Oh, I was so proud of you that day because you were the star, the leader, and you broke three school records and—" Her voice trailed off and a warm flush crept onto her cheeks. "I don't know why I'm going on and on about all this, for heaven's sake. It was a long time ago. As Trevor would say 'it's history.'"

"It's part of *our* history, Emily."

"Well, yes, I suppose it is," she said, averting her eyes from Mark's and fiddling with the pen. "But there's no purpose to be served by talking about it because we don't have a future together. Reminiscing about special memories is for people who... You know what I'm trying to say."

"Emily, I—"

"Mark," she interrupted, looking at him again, "did Trevor bring up the subject of whether you knew his father while the two of you were at the pool?"

"No," Mark said, shaking his head. "He didn't mention it at all. I told him, very casually, that I was built like him when I was his age and even through my high-school days, and that I filled out after I graduated. He lit up when he heard that news. I even said that I'd had an annoying cowlick like his and that I'd bet a buck that would be controlled once his hair thickened as he got older just as mine did.

"I'm just laying down some bricks in the foundation, Emily, so that he has this data when he learns that I'm his father. His mind isn't going off on a wild tangent of wondering why there are so many similarities between us. He believes that you and I were just friends in high school, nothing more."

Emily nodded.

"Trevor did spend quite a bit of time singing your praises, however," Mark went on. "I'm not entirely certain, but I think our son just might be attempting to do a bit of matchmaking."

"You're kidding," Emily said, her eyes widening. "Trevor is matchmaking, trying to get you and me… Oh, my stars!"

"Hey," Mark said, raising both hands, "I'm not sure about that, but pay attention to what he says and see if you agree with me."

"Trevor really does want a father, doesn't he? I obviously believed what was the most comfortable for *me,* buried my head in the sand. It's perfectly natural that a boy would want a dad.

"I can remember you telling me how you wished your father didn't drink all the time, would come to your swim meets, be a real dad for you instead of.... Oh, here I go again, traipsing down memory lane. I'm sorry. I don't mean to do that, Mark, I really don't."

"There's no harm in it," Mark said, lifting one shoulder in a shrug.

"Yes, there is. Everything is confusing and unsettling enough right now without—" Emily cleared her throat. "Yes. Well. I don't mean to be rude, but I really do need to finish this project so I can get it to the client. I appreciate you stopping by and letting me know how things went at the pool. I was certainly thinking about you. What I mean is, I was thinking about you and Trevor being together at the pool and wondering how it was going and... Thank you. Goodbye."

Mark chuckled and Emily narrowed her eyes, deciding it was his fault that a frisson of heat had slithered down her spine when he made that sexy sound, which he probably had been told by a multitude of women was a sexy sound, so he made that sexy sound on purpose, and—

"I'm getting a headache," she said, pressing one hand on her forehead.

"The remedy for that is spaghetti."

"Pardon me?"

"We're all going out for Italian food tonight. I told Trevor to pick the restaurant for dinner as a reward for following every directive I gave him as his pseudo coach and he chose Little Italy. Do they still make those terrific bread sticks?"

"Yes," Emily said, smiling, "and they still have the policy of all the bread sticks you can eat with your meal, even though you ate thirteen of them that night when we went there and… Oh, Emily, shut up."

Mark leaned over and dropped a quick kiss on Emily's lips.

"I do recall, Ms. MacAllister," he said, close to her lips, "that you ate your fair share of bread sticks that night, too. I'll pick you and Trevor up at six. See you later."

"Later," Emily said, then drew a quick breath as Mark straightened and strode toward the door.

As silence fell over the office once again, Emily placed the fingertips of one hand on lips that held the lingering taste of Mark's quick kiss.

Why had he done that? she thought wearily. Mark had kissed her goodbye as though it was the most expected and natural thing to do. It didn't make one bit of sense, darn him.

Why had he done that? Mark thought, as he drove away from the strip mall. He hadn't made a conscious decision to do it, he'd just up and kissed Emily goodbye because he'd been leaving and wouldn't dream of doing that without...well, kissing her goodbye. It must have been a leftover habit, plus the fact that they'd been reminiscing about eating a ridiculous number of bread sticks that night when they were teenagers.

"That explains it," Mark said nodding, as he maneuvered through the heavy traffic.

Except...

The bread sticks were then. That kiss had been now.

He'd been very aware of how lovely Emily had looked in the pretty summer blouse she'd been wearing. He'd also registered a rush of pride that she had her own business in a unique and challenging field. He'd kissed Emily goodbye because, damn it, he'd wanted to. Pure and simple. No, it was complicated as hell.

There he'd stood, telling Emily that they were going out to dinner to reward their son for his tireless efforts at the pool, and it had felt so right, so real, so warm. The Maxwell family was going out to eat.

But they weren't the *Maxwell* family. Trevor and Emily were MacAllisters and *he* was the lone Maxwell. He was the *lonely* Maxwell.

Mark parked in the lot of the hotel where he was staying, then folded his arms on top of the steering wheel and stared into space.

"Oh, hell, I'm in deep trouble," he muttered.

Ten minutes later he was stretched out on his bed in his hotel suite, hands beneath his head on the pillow, a deep frown on his face.

Emily, his mind echoed. Why couldn't he just focus on the incredible pain she had caused him years ago, hang onto the anger, the hurt, the betrayal that had nearly destroyed him?

Because that was then and this was now, and the Emily of today was so beautiful in her maturity. He couldn't help but be in awe of what she had done with her life in spite of being a single mother. She'd raised a terrific boy, had a dynamite career with endless potential, had worked so hard in the many roles she had. He respected her beyond measure for what she had done.

"Hey, Maxwell," he said aloud, "go with that one...what she had done."

She had kept the existence of his son from him, for God's sake. That was rotten to the core, really cold. If he hadn't come to Ventura he would never have known that Trevor was a living, breathing entity, which was more than Mark Maxwell was because Emily had killed him off and made him an angel in heaven, for cripe sake.

But...

Ah, hell, what choice had she had at the time but to do what she had done? She was expecting a baby. She'd realized that she was no longer in love with that baby's father. Did she hit on him to marry her, or go for beaucoup bucks for child support?

No.

And now that he knew of his son's existence? Emily was dealing with it with class.

Oh, yeah, Emily MacAllister was really something. Something rare, wonderful and special.

Mark smiled up at the ceiling. "I am woman, hear me roar."

She'd whipped that one on him, then laughed that sunshine laughter of hers, making her brown eyes sparkle with merriment. Emily was fun and funny, intelligent and beautiful.

She was obviously self-conscious about her weight, but to him it held no importance. So she was heavier than she'd been at eighteen. People change. Heaven knew he had.

Emily had loved him when he was a weird, geeky kid. He'd doubted that for a while, but he now knew in his heart that she had truly loved him. She never would have made love with him if she hadn't.

But Emily MacAllister had stopped loving Mark Maxwell.

And Mark Maxwell had never stopped loving Emily MacAllister.

Emily managed to finish the drawing, then called the client and made an appointment to deliver the report the next morning. She was straightening the supplies on the drafting table, preparing to head for home when Margaret MacAllister entered the office.

"Hi, Grandma," Emily said, smiling. "You almost missed me. My boss, me, said I'm finished for the day.'' She closed the distance between them and hugged her grandmother. ''It's good to see you, as always.''

''Hello, dear,'' Margaret said. ''I was hoping you'd still be here. I've been...well, worried about you.''

''Because of Mark Maxwell arriving in Ventura unannounced,'' Emily said, nodding. ''Let's sit down in the comfortable chairs. I've been leaning over a drafting table all day.''

The pair settled onto the chairs, then Margaret frowned as she met Emily's gaze.

''Emily, I won't deny that your grandfather and I always believed that Mark should have been told that he had a son.''

''I know. The entire family felt that way, but everyone respected my wishes.''

''Yes, we did. We were all so stunned by your announcement. Well, there's no sense in rehashing all of that. It was a long time ago. It was very apparent that Mark realized that Trevor is his son the moment he saw him in my living room,'' Margaret went on. ''I was glad, felt that Mark knowing about Trevor was long overdue, but since then I've been concerned about the entire situation.''

''I'm worried, too, Grandma. I'm terrified about how Trevor will react when he finds out the truth. Everything is so confusing and complicated. There's only one rather humorous thing in this whole crummy mess.''

''Which is?''

''The role reversal, of sorts. When Mark and I were in high school I was trim and slim, one of the pretty MacAllister triplets, and Mark was gangly and geeky. But now? Mark is drop-dead gorgeous, built like a dream, so confident and successful and I look like one of those Before pictures they use to advertise diet programs.'' She sighed. ''No, forget humorous. It's not funny at all, is it?''

''You stop that right now, Emily,'' Margaret said sternly. ''You're a very attractive woman. I don't want to hear you putting yourself down like that.'' She paused. ''Now then, tell me how Mark and Trevor are getting along.''

''Oh, famously,'' Emily said and proceeded to update her grandmother. ''I can't even imagine what Mark felt when he discovered he had a twelve-year-old son. Almost thirteen, as Trevor is quick to point out.''

Margaret frowned. ''The past has a way of catching up to us, doesn't it?''

So do lies, Emily thought miserably. ''Oh, brother,'' she said, ''wait until Mom and Dad get back from their trip up the coast and find out that Mark is here, knows about Trevor. My father is going to go ballistic, wondering if I'm all right, hovering around making sure that Mark isn't yelling his head off at one of Forrest MacAllister's baby girls.

The MacAllister triplets have a very protective daddy."

Margaret laughed. "That is certainly true, but it's because he loves you very much. We all do. By the way, I planted those flowers you brought to the house. They're absolutely lovely in that spot we prepared for them in my garden."

"Oh, gracious, I forgot all about them. I'm sorry."

"Don't give it another thought. You've had a great deal on your mind." Margaret got to her feet. "Well, I suppose the situation could be worse. What I mean is you and Mark don't have any…well, romantic feelings for each other, haven't had for over a dozen years, so you can both focus entirely on Trevor and what is best for your son."

Margaret looked at Emily intently.

"You don't, do you?" Margaret asked, raising her eyebrows. "Have any lingering feelings for Mark? It wouldn't be the first time that absence has made the heart grow fonder, or some such cliché."

"Grandma, Grandma," Emily said, getting up and hugging her. "You've been reading too many of those romance novels again."

"Mmm," Margaret said. "Well, I'm off. Do keep me posted, dear."

"Yes, of course, I will. I know you're worried about Trevor, just as I am. Give Grandpa a hug from me."

"I will," Margaret said, then crossed the room and left the office.

Emily sighed wearily and wrapped her hands around her elbows.

"I never stopped loving Mark Maxwell, Grandma," she whispered, tears echoing in her voice. "But I can't, won't, dwell on any feelings I might be having about him now, because he's so far out of my reach. My chubby little fingers' reach."

Six

The moment that Mark stepped into the restaurant with Emily and Trevor, memories swept over him like a nearly tangible warm and comforting cloak.

He smiled as he swept his gaze over the large room, remembering the night he'd brought Emily here to celebrate their being together for one year.

"Oh, hey," he said, tilting his head for a better look, "they've added a dance floor over there. Do they have live music? Do they play only Italian songs?"

"I forgot that you hadn't seen the addition to this place," Emily said. "They built it on a couple of years after you left Ventura. They have a combo that plays all kinds of music."

"Dorky stuff," Trevor said.

The hostess returned from seating a couple, then showed Emily, Mark and Trevor to a table set for four.

"You sit on that side with Mark," Trevor said to his mother. "I need lots of elbow room when I dive into spaghetti."

Mark assisted Emily with her chair, then bent over to speak close to her ear.

"Told you so," he whispered. "Matchmaking."

"Oh, good grief," Emily said.

"Good grief...what?" Trevor said.

"Good grief it smells heavenly in here," Emily said. "Spices, fresh bread... I'm gaining weight just sniffing the aromas floating through the air." She pushed her menu to one side and pointed a finger in the air. "But since I weighed myself after my shower and discovered I've lost another two pounds I'll hold myself back. A dinner salad and one bread stick. That's it for me."

"But this is a special event, Emily," Mark said. "We're celebrating the possibility that Trevor might be the next Olympic gold medalist. Can't you go off your diet tonight for this occasion?"

"Nope," Trevor said. "See, Mark, it's like this. My mom explained it to me. When you care about someone who's on a diet you don't do anything to sabotage their program. Know what I mean?" He leaned forward. "You *do* care about my mom, don't you, Mark?"

I'm in love with your mom, Trevor, Mark thought, meeting his son's gaze. *She's the only woman I have ever, or will ever, love.*

"Sure I do," Mark said, nodding. "I won't say another word about your mother ordering more food. Okay?"

"Good," Trevor said, then smiled. "I figured you cared about her because you've been friends since you were young, and now you're old and you're still friends. That's terrific."

"That's also enough, Trevor," Emily said. "Change the subject. Tell me about what you did at the pool today. Are you tired?"

"Wiped out," Trevor said, then yawned dramatically. "I'll need to hit the sack the minute we get home. You and Mark could rent a romantic Mom-and-Dad-type movie to watch—"

"You folks ready to order?" a waitress said, appearing at the table.

"We most certainly are," Emily said, glaring at Trevor, who produced a smile of pure innocence.

The orders were placed, then Emily urged Trevor once again to tell her about what he had done at the pool with Mark. Trevor launched into a report, hardly stopping to take a breath.

Mark was definitely right, Emily thought, only half listening to Trevor. Their son had begun a full-blown matchmaking campaign. Her baby boy had definitely missed not having a father all these years. It was so sad it made her heart ache.

Well, Trevor was going to get that father in the form of Mark Maxwell, but the end result would not be what Trevor was trying to make happen. His matchmaking number was a waste of time. There would be no happy little family of Mom, Dad and kiddo. Emily, Mark and Trevor. That wasn't going to happen.

"And, therefore," Trevor said, "I'm totaled. Might have trouble finding the energy to eat my dinner, which is headed this way even as I speak."

Before Emily could reply, the waitress served their orders and placed a basket of hot, fragrant bread sticks in front of Emily's placemat.

She and Mark had been celebrating their one-year anniversary when they'd eaten here, Emily suddenly remembered, staring at the bread sticks. That was the reason they'd gone out to dinner.

She'd worn a soft, fuzzy pink sweater over winter-white, form-fitting slacks. Mark had ironed, actually ironed, his best pair of jeans and added a pale-blue dress shirt.

His freshly shampooed hair had caused his cowlick to curl even more than usual, he'd knocked over a water glass and his napkin had slid off his lap three times during the delicious meal.

They'd felt so grown up that night, celebrating an anniversary the way mature, adult couples did. They'd talked about the children they'd create with exquisitely beautiful lovemaking. They'd even gone so far as to decide that they'd get a kitten and a puppy for the babies to play with.

So many dreams, Emily mused, her gaze still riveted on the bread basket.

Trevor's hand suddenly came into her view, his fingers wrapping around a bread stick, then removing it from the basket.

And one of those dreams had come true, Emily thought, shifting her gaze to her son. There was the miracle, the child created by the beautiful lovemaking shared with Mark. But the remainder of the hopes and dreams had been blown away like sand from the palm of an outstretched hand. Gone forever.

"Emily?" Mark said. "Is something wrong? You look rather unhappy."

"What?" she said, shaking her head slightly as she returned to the present. "Oh. No, I'm not... Well, yes, I'm pining away here, wishing I could grab a bread stick in each hand and gobble them up."

"Can't have that," Trevor said, reaching for the basket. He placed one bread stick on Emily's side plate, then set the basket at the other end of the table. "There you go, Mom. Out of sight, out of mind."

"That's an old saying, Trevor," Mark said, "but there are a great many things it doesn't apply to." Like Emily MacAllister. "Your spaghetti looks terrific there, kid. My lasagna is superb, too. How's your salad, Emily?"

Emily took a bite of the salad and nodded as she chewed and swallowed.

"Delicious. So. Mark. Tell us about your research work."

Mark laughed. "Bottom line? I'm out of a job. I'm among the unemployed at the moment. Oh, they'd find a spot for me in Boston as I was on a leave of absence when I went to Paris. But my place on my team had to be filled and there's nothing that interests me right now. Will you throw me a bread stick when I get to the point where I'm homeless and hungry?"

"You don't have to go back to Boston?" Trevor said, his eyes widening. "I asked you where you lived and you said Boston and I thought you— This is so radical. You can live wherever you want to? Like, say, here in Ventura?"

"It's not that simple, Trevor," Mark said, frowning. "I'm in research, which means I have to find a hospital or private company with funding for my type of expertise.

"I really haven't given it any thought since I arrived in Ventura because...because there were other things occupying my mind.

"Hey, I'm on vacation, and it has been years since I've taken any time off. Nobody wants to think about work while they're hanging out, you know what I mean?"

''Yeah, but couldn't you check it out?'' Trevor said. ''See if some place in Ventura has research bucks, or something?''

''Trevor,'' Emily said, ''Mark just told you that he's on vacation and doesn't want to dwell on work now.''

''But...'' Trevor said.

''Eat your spaghetti, Trevor,'' Emily said, ''before it gets cold.''

''But...''

''Trevor,'' Emily said firmly.

''Yeah, okay, I hear you,'' Trevor said, his shoulders slumping. ''But it just seems to me that... Okay, okay, I'm eating my spaghetti.''

The trio ate in silence for several minutes with Emily taking tiny little bites of the bread stick to make it last longer.

''Actually,'' Mark finally said, ''I've had an idea floating around in my weary brain since a couple of months after I arrived in Paris. It keeps popping up, forcing me to take a look at it.''

''What is it?'' Emily said, glancing over at him.

''Well, I have so much data in my head from the various research projects I've been involved with,'' Mark said, staring into space. ''The thing is, medical books are so high-tech that the average person can't understand anything much beyond the title page.

''What if a person wrote a book that was user-friendly, for lack of a better term? Say that Trevor wanted to do a report on DNA for his science class.

My book would be done in such a way that he could really understand DNA, or whatever the topic was. I would knock it all down into terms, diagrams and what have you, that a person of any age could understand."

"Cool," Trevor said, nodding. "Very cool. You could be an author like my Grandma Jillian, except she writes romantic stuff about pirates and people in the old days and..." He eyes widened. "My Grandma Jillian told me once that she can write wherever she remembers to take her brain with her... Oh, and her laptop computer. This is so radical, Mark. You could write a book here in Ventura."

Mark nodded slowly. "That would be the plan if I decided to go that route."

Mark was considering staying on in Ventura, living here? Emily thought, her mind racing. But... Well, yes, she guessed that made sense because his son was here.

Mark had already told her how he regretted missing out on so many years of Trevor's life. He apparently had no intention of missing out on the next thirteen, or the thirteen after that.

It had just never occurred to her that he might move here permanently. Good grief, that was a rather unsettling thought. But then again, it would mean she needn't worry about Trevor moving away to live with his father.

It had nothing to do with her, wouldn't affect her

day-to-day existence and Trevor would have the father he had been yearning for.

"I think that's a marvelous idea, Mark," Emily said, smiling.

"You do?" he said, looking over at her.

"Well, sure. You know all the MacAllisters due to the fact that you lived with my grandparents for all those months. You'd have a ready-made family to spend the holidays with, celebrate birthdays and you could go to Trevor's swim meets if he makes the team."

"Wouldn't you come to the swim meets, too, Mom?"

"Oh, well, of course, I would."

"Then you and Mark could come together to watch me swim," Trevor said, reaching for another bread stick. "Way cool."

"Let's not get ahead of ourselves. I know a guy in New York who's in publishing. I'd have to talk to him, have him check around and see if there would be a market for the kind of book I'm thinking of. That would be the first step."

"Can you call him tomorrow?" Trevor said.

Mark laughed. "Yeah, I'll call him tomorrow." He paused. "I would really like to have a break from research. It's very intense stuff, and it has a way of consuming me to the point that I get tunnel vision, focusing only on what I'm working on. I'd like to add..." He slid a glance at Emily, then looked at Trevor. "...other things to my life, have a fuller, more well-rounded existence for a change."

"I can understand that," Emily said quietly. "When I worked at home I narrowed down my life far too much. I'm much happier now that I have an office to go to. I see people, interact with them. My mother has always said that writing is a lonely business, that the author is the only person who can do it...alone."

"I'm sure that's true," Mark said. "But I know your mother. She's a vibrant, outgoing woman. She's always had her writing and life in good balance as far as I can see. I'd just have to pay attention to what I was doing and make sure I didn't become a recluse pounding away on my computer keys."

"Wouldn't happen," Trevor said. "You'd be a MacAllister, sort of. There's always something going on with the MacAllisters because our family is huge.

"Hey, you could get a smokin' deal on a house, too. We have tons of architects in the family, and my Uncle Andrew still owns his construction company even though he's retired. And a pool. Be sure and tell them you want a pool when they draw up the plans for your house."

"Whoa," Mark said, laughing. "You're going too fast here, Trevor. I can't take a couple of years to write a book that nobody wants to buy, you know."

"I'll buy it," Trevor said.

"Oh, well, that settles it then," Mark said, smiling. "No, seriously, I have to do my homework. Find out if there's a publisher interested in what is taking up my brain space. I'll keep you posted. Okay?"

"It'll fly," Trevor said. "I know it will." He snapped his fingers. "Badda-bing, badda-boom, sold. It's a done deal, guaranteed, you'll see."

"Ah, the faith of the young," Emily said, smiling as she looked at Mark.

"Who believe in hopes and dreams," Mark said, meeting her gaze.

"Yes," Emily said hardly above a whisper, unable to tear her gaze from Mark's.

Ah, Emily, Mark thought. What happened to our hopes and dreams, all our wonderful plans? What happened to the love you felt for me that was so rich, real and honest? What happened to it all, Emily?

"You folks ready for some dessert?" the waitress said, suddenly appearing by the table and causing Emily and Mark to jerk and direct their attention to her.

"No, thank you," Emily said, her voice unsteady.

She vaguely heard Mark and Trevor order gelato as she drew a much-needed breath.

Dear heaven, she thought frantically, she had felt such burning desire sweep throughout her when Mark had pinned her in place with those mesmerizing eyes of his.

But no, no, no, it hadn't been desire for *this* Mark. They had been talking about the faith of the young who believed in hopes and dreams.

Well, she'd passed the baton of that kind of believing on to her son, because her hopes and dreams were gone, had been blown away into oblivion. Forever.

The gelato arrived and was rapidly consumed by Mark and Trevor, with Emily averting her eyes from what she knew was a delicious dessert that was definitely not on her diet program.

"Filled to the brim," Trevor said, leaning back in his chair and patting his stomach. "I'm stuffed."

"So am I," Mark said.

"No comment," Emily said, smiling. "That gelato looked so good. I'll treat myself to a dish of it on my fortieth birthday, or some such thing."

"I'll remember that," Mark said, nodding. "One dish of gelato for your big four-oh."

"You'll still be around when Mom's that old?" Trevor said, staring at Mark.

"I'll be around, Trevor." Mark looked directly at his son. He pushed his empty ice-cream bowl to one side and folded his arms on the top of the table. "Listen, even if the book deal is a wash, I intend to stay on here. I'd see what kind of research projects are out there, or I could teach if it came to that.

"It all came together for me here, tonight, sitting at this table. Whatever it takes, I'm going to be living in Ventura."

Seven

Mark's declaration seemed to hover above the middle of the table and a silence fell over the trio. They each became centered on their own thoughts of what Mark's living in Ventura would mean to them.

A smile formed on Trevor's lips as he drew invisible patterns on his place mat with the spoon from his finished ice cream.

Mark slowly relaxed what he realized were tightened muscles in his body, then nodded in satisfaction as a sense of rightness about his abrupt decision suffused him. He leaned back in his chair, folded his arms across his chest and made no attempt to hide an expression of I'm-very-pleased-with-myself-thank-you-very-much.

Emily's shoulders slumped with weariness as she dealt with a cacophony of voices in her mind, telling her that having Mark stay on in Ventura would be fantastic for Trevor...once their son dealt with the truth of Mark being his father.

Telling her that Mark would probably buy a house, get settled in, and perhaps find a special woman to love and marry, perhaps even have more children.

Wouldn't that be nice? Emily thought. Sure. Trevor would be a marvelous big brother to a half sister or brother.

Oh, dear heaven, Mark holding, kissing, making love with a woman he'd declared his forever love to? Mark creating a little miracle, a baby, in the darkness of night with that woman? Mark actually living out, with someone else, all the hopes and dreams that had once been theirs?

She was hating this, she really was, which didn't make one bit of sense because this Mark, the one sitting only inches away from her, was the father of her child and nothing more. Not any longer.

Trevor suddenly straightened in his chair. "Here comes the combo. The dorky music is about to begin."

"What?" Emily said, then blinked back to attention. "Oh, well, we're finished here so we'll leave so you won't be subjected to the music, Trevor."

"No," Trevor said quickly. "I mean, hey, I'm

just sitting here vegging. I'm cool. You and Mark should go dance, Mom."

"Don't be silly," Emily said, pushing back her chair. "I haven't danced..."

"In far too long, I think," Mark said, rising and extending his hand to Emily. "Shall we?"

No, we shall not, Emily thought, staring at Mark's hand. She was not about to give Mark a hands-on demonstration of just how much more there was of said Emily these days. Not a chance. Nope. No way.

"Emily?" Mark said, his hand still close to her, palm up. "Please?"

Emily's breath caught as she saw her hand float up and land gently in Mark's, watched as his fingers curled around her hand, then felt herself being drawn up to stand next to him.

"Awright," Trevor said, making a fist and giving it a jerk in approval. "Go for it. I'll just sit here and digest my spaghetti. Don't rush back."

Emily stared at Trevor for a long moment as though she'd never seen him before in her life, then the next thing she knew she was walking next to Mark, who still had a firm hold on her hand, just as brazen as you please, toward the shiny dance floor.

She felt, Emily thought hazily, as though she were watching this ridiculous performance from some strange place outside herself and shaking her head in dismay as she witnessed Emily MacAllister about to allow Mark Maxwell to attempt to wrap his arm around her lumpy, bumpy, overweight blimp of a body.

This was, without a doubt, one of the dumbest, most humiliating things she'd ever done in her entire fat-adult life.

They stepped onto the dance floor. Mark turned and slid one hand to the back of Emily's waist. She stood statue-still, stiff as a pencil and stared at the center of his chest.

"I'm not going to bite you, Emily," Mark said quietly. "We're going to dance to this nice music. Okay?"

"Oh, I don't think..."

"Good. Don't think," Mark interrupted, pulling her close. "Just dance with me."

"But..."

"Shh," he said, then they began to sway to the lovely music lilting through the air. "Mmm. Your hair smells like flowers and sunshine."

That did it.

Emily gave up the battle, shut down the war raging in her mind, and just...danced.

With Mark.

The Mark...of now.

He was so tall, so strong, powerful, yet gentle, she thought dreamily. His body was so taut and so masculine, and his aroma of fresh air, soap and a woodsy aftershave suited him perfectly. He moved with such easy grace and was holding her as though she was delicate, special, the most important and most beautiful woman among all the couples surrounding them.

Oh, Mark.

Mark closed his eyes for a long, long moment to savor the feel of Emily pressed to his body and to inhale yet again her enticing feminine aroma.

This wasn't a teenager, a near-child he was embracing, he thought, this was a mature woman, whose lush breasts were crushed to his chest. Her body was fuller, befitting someone who had given birth to a child, and she felt like heaven itself in his arms.

If only, *only* she hadn't fallen out of love with him after he'd moved to Boston. He would have seen her grow big with their child. Trevor. He would have been there with, and for, his wife and son the way he should have been, providing for them, watching over and protecting them from harm. They would have been a real family, living in a house that had become a home filled with love and laughter and…

Yeah, right.

He would have been eighteen years old, without a penny in his pocket, with a wife and child to support. They would have had to live with Emily's parents, or grandparents, been taken care of like the children they were, who had a child of their own they couldn't buy food and clothes for.

The song ended and another dreamy tune started immediately.

Don't go there, Maxwell, Mark told himself. There was no point in looking back to the might-have-beens. What was important was now and the future.

What was *very* important was that he was holding Emily in his arms, and she was slowly but surely relaxing her stiff posture and allowing him to nestle her close to him.

How strange it all was. Years before when he'd been shorter and skinny as a post, all arms and legs and enormous feet, teenage Emily had seemed to be custom-tailored just for him. And now? He was much taller, had filled out, and Emily the woman felt as though she was custom-tailored just for him.

Heat. It was building, coiling, low in his body, Mark thought, rather hazily. Burning. He wanted Emily. He desired her as he had when he was a boy, but with the deeper intensity of the man he had become. He wanted to make love with this Emily through the private hours of the night, caress and kiss so gently, reverently, every inch of the woman *she* had become.

And he would want to declare his love for her as they became one, but that he would never do. Not again. Because Emily MacAllister didn't love *him*, hadn't loved him in many, many years. He would bury his feelings for her deep within himself and never allow the words that would reveal his emotions to be spoken.

Yes, he would move to Ventura, then learn to be

satisfied with just seeing Emily as he established a father-and-son relationship with Trevor. How bleak that all was in his mental vision. He'd go to sleep alone each night, wake up alone each morning, aching for the woman he loved who would never be his again.

He would move to Ventura…and still be lonely.

Don't think, Maxwell, Mark told himself sternly. Just feel. Just savor every second of holding Emily in your arms after so many long years.

Mark blanked his mind and danced.

Dear heaven, Emily thought, she was going up in flames of desire so intense her bones were going to dissolve and she'd disappear from the face of the earth, never to be seen again.

She wanted to make love with Mark Maxwell.

This was terrifying, unsettling her to the very depths of her inner being. Because she wanted to make love with the Mark of now, this Mark, the one who was holding her so tightly in his strong arms.

This Mark, who was so handsome and so masculine, so at ease with the incredible maleness he now possessed.

This Mark, who had achieved success in his chosen field far beyond what others had done at his age.

This Mark, who had already shown what a loving and devoted father he would be to his son.

This Mark, who was slowly but surely bringing her love for him in the past into the present.

Oh, Emily, don't do this, she silently begged herself. She mustn't allow this to happen. Mark was awakening emotions and desires within her that she'd put firmly to sleep years before. He was everything that had caused her to give him her heart and body with a sense of rightness, honesty and love.

But to love, be in love, with *this* Mark would result in her heart being broken into a million pieces. She was fat and unsophisticated, would never fit into the world Mark now existed in.

She must not let her feelings for Mark from then mesh into the seconds, minutes, hours, days of the now. He wouldn't want her. He'd reject her. Just as he believed she'd rejected him years before. The mere thought of it in her mind was so chilling, was so much more than she'd be able to bear.

But how did she stop it from happening? What button did she push? What handle did she turn? Where could she hide from the rekindled emotions and desires that were building steadily within her? She didn't know the answers to any of those questions. She just didn't.

Don't think anymore, Emily told herself. Not now. She'd deal with all of this…later. She was just going to dance…with Mark.

Time lost meaning.

The music played on.

And they danced.

As Mark turned Emily to the waltz the band was now playing, she registered, rather foggily, the fact that her grandparents were sitting at the table where she and Mark had left Trevor a zillion years ago.

That's nice, she thought dreamily. Trevor had someone to talk to while she was awash with desire for the man who was holding her so close to his body. Trevor could sit and chat with—

Emily stiffened, blinked, then came to such an abrupt halt that Mark stepped on her toe.

"My grandparents?" she said, looking up at Mark with wide eyes.

"What?" Mark said. He shook his head slightly to dispel the passion-laden mist that had consumed him, then frowned. "Who? Huh?"

"My grandparents are here," Emily said. "They're sitting at our table with Trevor. How long have we been gone from there? How many songs did we dance to? What time is it?"

"Emily, calm down," Mark said, as the other couples on the floor danced around them. "What are you getting so upset about?"

"Think about it, Mark. Can you even imagine what our son, the matchmaker, is in the process of telling my grandparents at this very minute? We've been dancing forever, and you were holding me so close, and I had my head nestled on your shoulder...when did I do that?...and we must have looked like...like..."

Mark grinned. "Like what?"

"This is *not* funny," she said, stepping out of his embrace.

"It's not the end of the world, either. So...we danced. A lot. So...yes, okay, I held you close, very close, and it was wonderful."

"Oh, I know, I know," Emily said, staring into space with a smile on her lips. "It was heavenly, and I..." Her eyes widened again. "We've got to get back to that table and nip this in the bud."

Emily marched from the dance floor with Mark following more slowly behind her.

Sensational, Mark thought, unable to curb his smile. Emily was all aflutter, with her hands doing their butterfly thing and her cheeks flushed such a pretty pink. She was off and running, determined to do damage control on Trevor's matchmaking.

Trevor's matchmaking, Mark's mind echoed, as he slowed his step even more. What if it worked? What if it honest-to-goodness worked, and Emily fell back in love with him? Trevor might be enlisting the help of his great-grandparents in his scheme? Oh, go for it, son. The father in this scenario needed all the help he could get.

Was it possible?

Could it really happen?

He didn't have a clue, but he sure as hell was going to do his part in what was unfolding here. And he was going to be paying very, very careful attention to what Emily said and did.

Was he setting himself up to be cut off at the knees again? Yes, there was a very good chance that was exactly what would happen. Emily had stopped loving him years ago. All the fancy matchmaking ever invented might not be able to rekindle love that was dead, cold and buried. Forgotten.

But if he didn't declare his love to Emily, he at least wouldn't look like a fool if Trevor's matchmaking fizzled. He'd maintain his dignity. He had nothing to lose and there was a chance—albeit very, very remote—that he had everything to gain that he had ever wanted.

Game on, Mark thought, as he stopped at the table where the group was gathered.

"Good to see you, Mark, and haven't you turned into a fine-looking man," Robert MacAllister said, getting to his feet and shaking Mark's hand. "I've been looking forward to this moment ever since Margaret told me you were vacationing in Ventura."

"Cancel vacationing," Trevor said. "Mark is going to live here permanently."

"Oh?" Margaret and Robert said in unison, looking at Mark with obvious interest.

"Excuse me," the waitress said, from behind Mark. "I have three desserts to deliver to hungry folks."

Mark stepped out of her way, Robert sat back down, and dishes of ice cream were set in front of Margaret, Robert and Trevor.

"Trevor?" Emily said. "You ordered another dish of ice cream?"

"Gelato," Trevor said, nodding. "A guy can never get enough gelato. I got hungry again sitting here while you and Mark danced to about fifty lame songs.''

"It wasn't fifty,'' Emily said. Or maybe it was. She had no idea at this point. "Well, I guess we could find another chair and all crowd in here while we wait for you to eat that.''

"That won't be necessary, dear,'' Margaret said pleasantly. "Robert and I suddenly had the urge to have some of this delicious ice cream, then joined Trevor when we saw him sitting here alone. We'd like Trevor to spend the night with us so he can help me rearrange my living-room furniture tomorrow. I'll drive him to the community center when we're finished.''

"You rearranged your living room last week,'' Emily said, frowning.

"It's out of balance,'' Margaret said. "Every time I walk into that room I feel as though it's going to tip over because there are too many of the bigger pieces of furniture on one side. It needs to be redone, and Trevor has graciously offered to assist me.''

"Yep, I did,'' Trevor said, then took a big bite of ice cream.

"Grandpa,'' Emily said, narrowing her eyes, "didn't you lend a hand in arranging the lopsided room? As in, you could help fix it?''

"That's true, sweetheart,'' Robert said, "but I have a golf date. I'd be much too tired to lug furniture around after playing eighteen holes.''

"Since when?'' Emily said. "The last time you

played eighteen holes of golf you came home and took Grandma out to dinner and a movie.''

''At my age you have good days and bad days,'' Robert said, then sighed dramatically. ''I'm in the midst of a week of weary, weak days.''

''Oh, you are not,'' Emily said.

''Yes, he is,'' Margaret said quickly. ''I had to go outside and get the newspaper from the walk this morning because your grandfather was too tired to make the trek. Bad days just sneak up on you at our age, dear.''

''Mmm,'' Emily said.

''So, therefore,'' Margaret said, ''there's no need for you and Mark to wait for Trevor—don't eat so fast, Trevor, or you'll get an ice-cream headache—to finish his dessert. You two just run along and Trevor will come home with us. Just remember to pick him up at the community center tomorrow afternoon because he won't have his bike.''

''I'll do the same swimming routine tomorrow that you put me through today, Mark,'' Trevor said. ''Bye, Mom. Bye, Mark. See you tomorrow.''

''Here's your purse, Emily,'' Margaret said, picking it up off the floor. ''Good night.''

''It's great to have you back in Ventura, Mark,'' Robert said. ''By the way, you look lovely this evening, Emily. Goodbye.''

Mark chuckled and Emily snapped her head around and glared at him as the sexy sound caused the now-familiar frisson of heat to slither down her spine.

"I believe we've been dismissed," Mark said, then reached for the dinner check that was on the table. "Shall we go?"

"But..."

"Say good-night, Emily," Mark said.

"Good night, Emily," she said, a rather bemused expression on her face.

"Ta-ta, darlings," Margaret said. "Now then, Trevor, tell us all about this swimming regimen that Mark has set up for you."

Mark placed his hand in the middle of Emily's back and steered her to the front of the restaurant. He paid the bill, then took her hand in his and led her from the building. It wasn't until they were in the vehicle and driving in the busy traffic that she finally spoke again.

"They're in on it," she said, folding her arms over her breasts. "That's what was going on in there. My grandparents came to the restaurant for ice cream, Trevor snagged them and recruited them as part of his matchmaking scheme. I'm telling you, Mark, Margaret and Robert MacAllister are in cahoots with my...our son."

Mark nodded. "I'd say that you've come to an accurate conclusion there, Ms. MacAllister. What a riot."

"It's not funny," Emily said, nearly yelling.

"Sorry," Mark said, cringing. "I just think it's rather humorous myself."

"No, it's not. It's terrible. Just awful." Emily sighed. "Trevor wants a father so badly he's rounding up the troops in an attempt to get one...you. It just breaks my heart because I didn't know he felt so strongly about this."

"Hey, take it easy," Mark said. "Don't start beating yourself up about this, Emily. Mark is going to get the father he wants...me. Everything is going to be fine once he adjusts to the facts, the...truth."

"But he wants a storybook family, don't you see? Papa bear, Mama bear and Baby bear, that sort of thing."

Ditto, Mark thought.

"Well," Emily went on, "some is better than none, I guess. Trevor getting the father that he has yearned for will, I hope, make it easier to put aside any anger he might feel when he finds out I've lied to him his entire life.

"'Hey, kid, remember that angel-in-heaven-father I told you about? Well, guess what? He lost his wings, got booted out and here he is in the flesh...your dad.' Oh, good grief, what a mess I've made of everything."

"Emily, come on, cut it out. You did what you felt was right at the time."

"And let's remember how torqued you were when you found out what I did."

"Okay, but I've cooled off now, understand that

you made decisions with the best of intentions. In my opinion they were crummy choices, but…" He shrugged. "What's done is done, and it's going to be corrected. Everything will be just fine."

"Mmm," she said, frowning.

"Emily, please," Mark said, glancing over at her, then redirecting his attention to the traffic, "don't ruin what has been a terrific evening by getting upset. I had a great time tonight. Did you?"

"I…" Emily turned her head to look out the side window. "Yes. Yes, I did." A rather terrifying, unsettling, confusing time but… "It was lovely, very…nice and…"

"Special," Mark said quietly.

"And special," she said softly.

They drove the remaining miles to Emily's house in silence, each lost in their own thoughts.

In Emily's living room she snapped on a lamp, then turned to face Mark, aware that she was suddenly very nervous and uncomfortable.

This moment, she thought, was like the end of a real date, just like in the movies, or in one of the romance novels her mother wrote. She'd only been out on a few dates since Mark left Ventura so many years before. Darn it, she couldn't remember what she was supposed to say now.

"I had a lovely time this evening, and I thank you very much," Emily said, staring at a spot about two inches above Mark's head.

"You're welcome," Mark said, standing in front of the closed door. "I enjoyed myself, too. Very much."

"Right." Emily nodded. "Well. So. I guess I'll just say good night then. Would you be free to pick up Trevor at the community center tomorrow about four o'clock? I have a client coming in at four-thirty. Trevor will be fine here alone for an hour or so."

Mark nodded. "Sure, no problem, but why don't we all go out for hamburgers after you get home from work? Then you won't have to cook after a long day at your office."

"Okay. That's dandy. Thank you," she said, then wrapped her hands around her elbows. "So. Well. Um... Oh, good grief."

"Emily," Mark said, frowning, "am I making you nervous? Edgy? Upset? What? Give me a hint here."

"Well, for Pete's sake, Mark," she said, none too quietly, "of course I'm a wreck. This is weird. I mean, this is like being brought home from an honest-to-goodness date, and I'm supposed to know what to say and do, and I don't, because I don't have oodles of experience doing this like you do, and I feel really, really dumb and unsophisticated, and that makes me mad...and sad at the same time, and..." She sniffled and shook her head.

Mark closed the distance between them and gripped Emily's shoulders as she stared at the floor.

"Look at me."

"No."

"Emily, look...at...me."

She raised her head slowly and Mark nearly groaned aloud when he saw the tears shimmering in her big, brown eyes.

"I'm sorry. I'm suffering from mental overload at the moment because so much has happened so quickly. I'm overreacting to being delivered home to my very own living room. I mean, what did I think you'd do? Leave me in the front yard? Ignore my foolishness, please, Mark, and just go. Try to erase from your memory bank the fact that I'm acting like a jerk."

"You're not a jerk. I think you're acting like a woman who has centered her life on raising her son alone and establishing a career. A woman who hasn't taken time for herself in a long while. There's nothing foolish or jerky about that. That fact that you don't play the singles game is endearing, very sweet, nice."

"Dorky," Emily said, then sniffled again.

"No, it's not," Mark said firmly. "Look, the rules are that you ask me if I'd like some coffee. I say no thank you, it would keep me awake. We already have our plans set up for tomorrow night so that's covered. So, that only leaves one thing left to do."

"I'll walk you to the door," Emily said. "Okay. Got it. Off we go to the door."

"No, that's not it. In my attempt to bring you up

to snuff about the dating arena, I've used a method of show-and-tell. I've done the tell part. I'm moving right along to show now."

Mark lowered his head toward Emily's, slowly, very slowly.

Emily MacAllister, she mentally yelled at herself, *run like hell!* Mark, *this* Mark, the Mark of *now,* was about to kiss her and that was so dangerous it was scaring the bejeebers out of her. *Emily? Are you listening to yourself? Don't let this happen. No, no, no.*

Mark's mouth melted over Emily's in a gentle kiss that intensified in the next instant as he parted her lips and slipped his tongue into the sweet darkness beyond.

Oh, yes, yes, yes, Emily thought.

As Emily's arms floated upward to encircle Mark's neck, he shifted his to her back, and she allowed herself to be nestled against him. He raised his head a fraction of an inch to take a sharp breath, slanted his mouth in the opposite direction and claimed her lips once again.

Desire exploded within them with licking flames, consuming them, rendering them incapable of rational reasoning. They could only feel, savor. Want.

Emily, Mark's mind thundered along with his heart. It had been a lifetime since he'd kissed her. No, it had been a second ago because he knew this sweet nectar taste of her, and her feminine aroma, and the intensity of his need, the burning passion that only she could produce in his aching body, because she was Emily.

And he loved her.

Mark broke the kiss and spoke close to Emily's slightly parted lips.

"I want you," he said, his voice gritty. "I want to make love with you, Emily, so damn much."

"I want you, too, Mark," she whispered, then wondered absently who had said that, and who that was who was taking Mark's hand and leading him across the living room, down the hall and into her bedroom.

The lamp in the living room cast a muted, rosy glow over the bedroom as Emily swept back the blankets on the bed, then moved eagerly back into Mark's embrace to receive and return a searing kiss in total abandon.

A whimper of need caught in Emily's throat.

A groan of want rumbled in Mark's chest.

He ended the kiss and reached for the buttons on Emily's blouse, his hands not quite steady. One button, two, three were undone, then Emily stiffened suddenly, her eyes widening as she took a step backward, clutching the edges of her blouse over her full breasts.

"Wait," she said, an edge of panic in her voice. "Close the door."

Mark frowned in confusion. "We're the only ones in the house, Emily."

"Then go turn off the lamp in the living room,"

she said, feeling the color draining from her face. "I can't deny that I want you, want to make love with you. I can't. But I'm not the Emily I used to be, and the thought of you seeing... How could you possibly desire a woman who is...is...fat and lumpy and..." Tears choked off her words and a chill of soul-deep misery consumed her.

"How could you have desired a boy," Mark said, "who was built like a skinny stick, was uncoordinated, had feet like gunboats and a cowlick that made him look like a cartoon character?"

"None of that mattered," she said. "You were Mark."

"And you are Emily and I want to make love with you. Do you think I'm so shallow that your weighing a few more pounds than before makes a difference to me? I like how you look. You're a woman grown, who has given birth to my son. You're beautiful, Emily. You're special, rare, wonderful and so beautiful you take my breath away." He opened his arms. "Come to me. Please."

And she went.

Feeling special, rare, wonderful and beautiful, Emily flung herself into Mark's embrace, tears brimming her eyes as she felt a glorious sense of rightness, of being where she belonged after such a long, long time away.

Mark kissed her deeply, then they removed their clothes, their eyes sweeping over the other, seeing and cherishing the changes, savoring the sight of the familiar.

They tumbled onto the bed, each reaching for the other, kissing, caressing, rediscovering what they had never really forgotten. Mark splayed one hand on Emily's rounded stomach, and she stiffened again as images of the slender girl she had once been flashed in her mental vision.

"Our son grew in here," Mark said, trailing a ribbon of kisses along Emily's neck, causing her to shiver at the same time as the heat low in her body increased its intensity. "Our miracle that we created together. Thank you, my beautiful lady, for Trevor."

"Oh-h-h," Emily said, sniffling, then relaxed again, giving way to her rising passion.

Mark laved the nipple of one of Emily's full breasts with his tongue, and she closed her eyes to savor the exquisite sensations swirling within her. He moved to the other breast to pay homage to the sweet bounty.

Emily's hands skimmed over Mark's back, marveling at the taut muscles bunching beneath her palms. When he sought her lips again, she sank her fingers into his thick hair, then pressed his mouth harder onto hers. Their tongues met in the darkness of her mouth, dueling, dancing, heightening their desire to a fever pitch.

They kissed, touched, hands never still, lips going where hands had traveled, leaving a moist, heated path in their wake. So hot. Burning. Until they could bear no more.

"Oh, Mark, please," Emily said, a sob catching in her throat.

"Yes. I want to protect you, Emily. Wait for me."

Forever, Emily thought dreamily, as Mark moved off the bed. She *had* waited for Mark, for all these years, and now he was home again...with her.

Mark returned to the bed, moved over Emily and into her, gently, slowly, watching her face for any hint that he was hurting her, knowing it had been years since he'd left her, glorying in the fact that there had been no other man sharing this intimate act with her while he'd been gone.

Emily gripped Mark's shoulders as he filled her. She was awed by the strength and power of all he was bringing to her. He began the rhythm, and she met him beat for beat as he increased the tempo to a thundering cadence.

Heat coiled low in their bodies as they approached the release, the place where they could only go together. Higher. Hotter. Lifting up and away until they were flung into the wondrous oblivion of sparkling colors they had sought.

They hovered in ecstasy, then seemed to float back down in a swaying motion that was gentle and peaceful and brought them back to reality with a soothing touch.

Mark shifted off Emily, then kept her close to his side as he sifted the fingers of one hand through her silky hair. She flattened one hand on his chest, feeling the moist curls of the hair there and the muscles beneath.

Oh, mercy, Emily thought, she was in love with this man. *This* man. Had never *stopped* loving him. She'd buried her feelings so deep within her that she hadn't even known they were there, but now there was nowhere to hide from the truth of her love for Mark Maxwell. But she could not, would not, tell Mark how she felt.

"That was fantastic," Mark said quietly. "I didn't hurt you, did I?"

"No, oh, no. It was wonderful and..." She would cherish the memories of this night forever. "Wonderful."

"I think I'd better leave."

"I don't want you to go."

"I don't want to go, believe me," he said, then kissed her on the forehead. "I want to wake up next to you in the morning and make sweet love to you again and again. But I..."

Emily sighed. "No, I know you're right. Trevor mustn't find out that we... Thank you, Mark, for making me feel so beautiful."

"You *are* beautiful, Emily."

He kissed her, long and deeply, causing the smoldering embers of desire within them to begin to glow, threatening to burst into raging flames once again.

"Nope," Mark said, chuckling, "I'm out of here

before I can't bring myself to leave. I'll see you here tomorrow night when you arrive from work. Trevor and I will be waiting for you to come home. Good night, lovely Emily. Sleep well."

"Good night, Mark," Emily whispered.

Mark left the bed and dressed quickly. He bent down, dropped a quick kiss on Emily's lips, then strode from the room. Darkness fell as he turned off the lamp in the living room, then Emily heard the quiet click of the front door close behind him.

And then she cried.

She rolled onto her stomach, buried her face in the pillow and cried.

She cried because for one fantasy-filled night she had been beautiful.

She cried because she now knew that she had never stopped loving Mark Maxwell, and it was so heartbreaking because he would never again love her as he once had.

She cried because she was fat, and a world apart from the sophisticated arena Mark existed in and she wished that she wasn't.

She cried because she was so scared of what would happen when Trevor was told of her mountain of lies.

Emily cried until exhaustion claimed her, and then she slept and dreamed of Mark.

Eight

This day, Emily thought, in the middle of the next afternoon, was a disaster due to the fact that she, the person who was attempting to function in it, was a basket case.

There was a never-ending ping-pong game being played in her brain, she mentally rambled on, pressing one fingertip to her forehead.

Ping...the memories of the lovemaking shared with Mark last night caused a warm flush to stain her cheeks and a soft smile to materialize on her lips.

Pong...making love with Mark had been a terrible mistake because it had caused the adolescent love she'd had for him years before to zoom into the present and consume her, the woman she was now.

She'd been walking around in a fog since she'd left the house that morning, she mused. She'd gotten halfway to her client's home to deliver the historical report she'd finished, when she'd realized she'd left it on the drafting table at the office.

At noon she'd ordered a salad to be delivered from the deli in the mall, only to remember as she ate it that she'd packed a salad at home and brought it with her.

She'd completely forgotten that this was the day to attend her tailor-made exercise class at the health club that went along with her diet. And only minutes ago she'd discovered that she was wearing one brown shoe and one black one. So, on top of being late for her appointment, she'd looked like someone who didn't know how to dress herself once she finally got there.

Enough of this pity party, Emily told herself. She was going to breeze into the house, greet Trevor and Mark, then off they'd go for hamburgers, which meant she would consume yet another salad. Mark would not have one clue, not the tiniest hint, that she was falling apart.

She could do this. She had to.

She'd worked too hard at building her sense of worth, her self-esteem after her grandfather had given her that exquisite, special mirror. She wasn't going to destroy all that she'd accomplished in regard to believing in herself, liking who she was.

"I am woman," she yelled, just as the door to the office opened.

"Cool," a teenager said. "What I need is for you to be the woman I'm supposed to deliver these flowers to."

Emily's eyes widened as she stared at the gorgeous bouquet of long-stemmed red roses in a crystal vase that had a red satin bow tied around it.

"Sorry, kiddo," she said. "You've got the wrong I-am-woman. Those sure aren't meant for me."

"Are you—" The boy looked at a clipboard he pulled from beneath his arm. "—Emily MacAllister?"

"Yes, but..."

"Bingo," he said, crossing the room and handing the vase to Emily. "Sign here."

Emily juggled the vase, scribbled her name on the appropriate line, then told the boy to wait while she got him a tip.

"It's been covered," he said, heading back toward the door. "Enjoy your posies."

"But..."

Emily frowned, slid off the high stool and walked to the desk where she could set the vase on a flat surface. She pulled a small white envelope free of what looked like a plastic fork and withdrew the card inside.

She felt the color drain from her face, then in the next instant it returned tenfold, causing her cheeks to flush with warmth.

"Emily," she read aloud, her voice quivering and her heart racing, "thank you for a special night. You *are* beautiful. Mark."

She leaned over and buried her nose in one of the luscious blossoms, then straightened and stared at the bouquet.

She had, she thought, at thirty-one years old, just received her first bouquet of flowers from a man.

Oh, they were such pretty flowers, but they were even more than that. Mark knew, just somehow knew, that she would be nervous about seeing him again, so he'd stepped up and taken care of the situation. He was letting her know with the delivery of this bouquet that he didn't regret what they had shared.

He didn't?

And he was even stating on this day after the deed that she was beautiful?

Was this confusing? Emily thought, frowning. It certainly was. Well, she'd just throw it on top of the heap of other confusing things in the maze in her mind, forget about it for now and thoroughly enjoy her lovely roses.

The telephone on the desk rang, causing Emily to jerk at the sudden noise. She snatched up the receiver.

"Then and Now," she said, in her cheerful telephone voice. "May I help you?"

"Emily? Hi, this is Jessica."

"Hello, sister mine. How are you? And Daniel? And Tessa?"

"We're all fine and dandy," Jessica said. "Listen, I signed up to do the family birthday bash for July, but since Daniel and I are still living in his apartment and can't smush everyone in there, we're borrowing Grandma and Grandpa's house. Daniel and I will take the cake and stuff over to their place.

"I realize this is Thursday and we're planning this shindig for Sunday at one o'clock, which is short notice, but I've been so busy with my court cases that the week just flew by."

"I imagine that happened to Perry Mason a lot, too," Emily said, smiling.

"No doubt about it. He told me that very thing," Jessica said, laughing. "Anyway, it's the usual routine. No gifts or we'd all be bankrupt, just cards for everyone with a July birthday, and it's potluck. Would you bring some kind of salad?"

"You have no idea what an expert I am at salads," Emily said. "Okay. I'll make a humongous salad to feed the multitudes of MacAllisters and sundry others."

"Speaking of others," Jessica went on, "I heard that Mark Maxwell is back in town and spending time with you and Trevor. A little birdie also whispered in my ear that Mark is now a real hunk of handsome stuff."

"Does that little birdie happen to be named Margaret MacAllister?"

"Emily, I'm an attorney who never divulges her sources of information."

"That's the code for journalists and police officers, Jessica," Emily said. "Your sworn-to-silence thing only covers your clients. I doubt seriously that Grandma hired you."

"Whatever," Jessica said merrily. "The point is, this invitation is extended to Mark, as well as to you and Trevor. Everyone will enjoy seeing him again."

"Oh, but..." Emily said, her mind racing.

"Oops, I have a call on another line that I've been waiting for. Gotta go," Jessica said. "Oh, before I forget. Mom and Dad will be back late Saturday night from their romp up the coast so they'll be attending the party."

"They weren't due back for another week or so," Emily said, her eyes widening.

"I know, but it's been raining like crazy up there and they decided to cut their trip short and come home in time for the July birthday basheroo. See you Sunday. Bye for now."

"But..." Emily said, then realized she was talking to the dial tone.

Emily replaced the receiver, then moved around the desk and sank onto the chair behind it as she spread her hands on her cheeks.

Dear heaven, she thought frantically, this was terrible, just awful, a complete and total disaster. There were just too many MacAllisters, too many chances of someone slipping and commenting on how much

Trevor looked like Mark had back when he was in high school.

"Oh, God," Emily whispered. "Trevor mustn't find out the truth like that, not like that."

Well, okay, so she wouldn't ask Mark to go to the party. That was simple enough. Right? Wrong. One of the mighty matchmakers would no doubt be certain that Mark received his warm-welcome invitation.

There was only one solution to this dilemma. Trevor had to be told the truth about Mark being his father before one o'clock on Sunday afternoon.

When Emily pulled into her driveway she saw a billow of smoke rising from the rear of the house.

"Oh, my God, the house is on fire," she shrieked, flinging the car door open.

She ran through the gate to the backyard and around the side of the house, only to stop dead in her tracks. Mark and Trevor were standing by the barbecue grill, waving their arms through the smoke that rose from the wobbly grill. She closed the distance between them, then coughed as she inhaled a mouthful of smoke.

"What—" Emily coughed again, then patted herself on the chest as she took a step backward out of the cloud of smoke. "What is going on here?"

Mark and Trevor emerged from the haze, looked at each other and burst into laughter.

"We were going to surprise you by making dinner ourselves, instead of going out,'' Mark said. ''We're grilling hamburgers that have just turned into hockey pucks. I think it probably goes without saying that I've never barbecued before.''

''I wouldn't make it your life's work if I were you,'' Trevor said, blinking several times. ''Man, that smoke is wicked.''

Emily smiled. ''Well, it's the thought that counts, gentlemen. I appreciate your efforts.''

''We bought all the trimmings to go with these hamburgers,'' Mark said, ''and there's more ground meat in the kitchen that we didn't kill. Why don't I just fry some burgers on the stove? *That* I know I can do.''

''Sounds good to me. I'll go change my clothes.''

Mark swept his gaze over Emily, then did a double take when he reached her feet. ''Love the shoes.''

Emily peered down at the black shoe and the brown one. ''It's a new fashion statement. You were out of the country so long, Mark, that you're not up-to-date on the latest fads here.''

''Yeah, right, Mom.''

''Got some beachfront property in Arizona you want to sell me, Emily?''

''You bet. I'll be back in a flash.''

''Wait a second, Emily,'' Mark said. ''I need you to show me where you keep the frying pan. Trevor, to put safety first, stay here until the fire in that monster goes out. I think that's the best way to handle it, rather than hosing it down."

"Okay," Trevor said.

In the kitchen Emily turned to face Mark.

"Thank you for the lovely flowers. I left them at the office because Trevor would go matchmaking nuts if he knew about them. It was so thoughtful of you to send them to me, and what you said on the card was lovely. I…I was afraid that you regretted… What I mean is, well, the flowers spoke for you."

"I have no regrets about last night, Emily," Mark said quietly, looking directly into her eyes. "I wanted to let you know that. Do you? Have regrets?"

"No, oh, no, not at all. It was wonderful and… Well, it complicated things, but… No, I'm not sorry that we…you know."

"Complicated things?" Mark said, frowning.

"Never mind. The frying pan is in the bottom cupboard there at the left of the sink. I'm going to go change into my jeans."

"Hold it just a minute."

He glanced out the sliding glass doors leading to the backyard where Trevor was doing push-ups on the grass beyond the smoke from the barbecue grill. He closed the short distance between him and Emily and framed her face in his hands.

"Welcome home," he said, then lowered his head and kissed her.

It's great to be here, Emily thought, as her lashes

drifted down and heat zinged throughout her. Oh, my stars, to think she hadn't wanted to come home. Oh, Mark.

Mark broke the kiss and drew a ragged breath. "Whew. You are potent stuff, madam. Go."

"Gone," Emily said, then pressed one hand to her forehead for a moment. "Gracious."

She hurried from the kitchen, and Mark watched her go until she disappeared from his sight.

"Welcome home, my love," he said, then moved to the proper cupboard and retrieved the frying pan.

A few minutes later, hamburger patties were sizzling in the frying pan on the stove.

Man, this was nice, Mark thought, staring at the browning meat. This was the stuff of which families were made. They came together at the end of the day and everyone pitched in to get dinner on the table. They'd chat as they ate, each sharing their news, caring about how the day had gone for those they loved. This was part of what changed a house into a home.

This was the lifestyle he wanted.

With Emily.

With Trevor.

With a baby in a high chair, merrily banging on the tray with a spoon.

With a dog curled up at his feet and a cat perched on the top of the refrigerator like the king in charge of the whole group.

Oh, yes, this was what he wanted and if he was

blessed enough to actually get it, earn it, he'd never again be lonely.

"Fire is out," Trevor said, coming in the back door. "Well, the one outside is. Why is there so much smoke coming from that frying pan?"

"Oh, cripe," Mark said, lifting the pan off the burner. "My mind wandered. These burgers are okay, thank goodness. Set the table, buddy."

Emily returned, dressed in jeans that were slightly too big and a short-sleeved, pink string sweater. A short time later, the trio was consuming their dinner, Emily agreeing to eat a hamburger patty with no bun, five potato chips and yet another salad.

Trevor gave a report on his swimming workout, then Mark said he'd spoken to his friend in New York who worked in the publishing industry.

"He knows an agent he's going to talk to about my ideas for the book," Mark said. "In the meantime, I should write a sample chapter, plus a cover letter stating what my credentials are and the general concept of what I plan to put together."

"How exciting," Emily said, leaning forward. "So you're really going to do it?"

"I'll give it my best shot," Mark said, nodding. "My friend said he thought it would fly...bigtime." He winked at Trevor. "I told him I'd already gotten a promise from a customer to buy a copy."

"Yep," Trevor said, then reached for another hamburger from the platter. "Good burgers, Mark. Finally."

"The best things are worth waiting for," Mark said, then looked at Emily, who immediately blushed a pretty pink and directed her attention to her plate.

They ate in silence for several minutes.

"I have news," Emily said finally, feeling a chill course through her. "We're all invited to the MacAllister July birthday party, Sunday at one o'clock. Jessica signed up for this month's bash, but it's being held at Grandma and Grandpa's house.

"Jessica said everyone will be delighted to see you again, Mark, after all these years. You know, the MacAllisters who knew you when you looked...very...different than you do now?" She stared at Mark intently.

Mark frowned and nodded slowly. "Yes, I understand what you're saying, but..."

"I can't go to that party, Mom. I'm spending Saturday night at Jacob's. It's his thirteenth birthday and his folks are taking us to dinner and a movie, then on Sunday to a picnic at Water World. We bought Jacob's present a couple of weeks ago, remember? I still have to wrap it, but you and Mark can go to the MacAllister party together so everything is cool."

"Very cool," Mark said. "Some things are worth waiting for, other things *definitely* shouldn't, and won't, be rushed."

"Huh?" Trevor said.

"Yes, now I recall that you have plans for the

weekend, Trevor,'' Emily said. ''I did forget, but that's fine. The family will understand.''

And *she* understood, she thought, what Mark had just alluded to. He'd gotten her message. Well, she could view this as a temporary reprieve, she supposed. It was just that ever since she'd decided to tell Mark the real reason she'd broken things off with him after he went to Boston, the lie was suddenly so heavy, it seemed to be crushing her with its weight.

Even though Mark would never know how she felt, the old lie didn't belong in what they were sharing in the present.

Saturday night, Emily thought. Trevor would be at Jacob's house. She and Mark could be alone. On Saturday night, she would tell Mark the truth about the letter of lies she written to him over a dozen years ago.

Nine

On Saturday, Emily cleaned the house, shopped for groceries, then later in the afternoon went to a stationery store with list in hand and bought cards for everyone in the family who had a July birthday. As she selected the last one she needed, she stared into space.

How should they sign the cards? she mused. Would Mark feel uncomfortable about not having any to pass out to the birthday people if she didn't include his name on the cards from her and Trevor? Or would it be presumptuous on her part to add his name? Well, phooey, she didn't know. So, she'd just ask Mark what he wanted to do.

As Emily reached the door to leave the store, a man entered and immediately smiled at her.

"Hello, Emily," he said.

"Oh, hello, Mr. Anderson," Emily said. "I haven't seen you in ages."

"It has been a long time," he said, nodding. "I've stopped in here to buy my wife an anniversary card. We've been married thirty-five years. I can't believe it's been that long."

"How lovely. Congratulations."

"Time has a way of flying by, doesn't it?" Mr. Anderson said. "It's seems like only yesterday that I was teaching English to you and your sisters, and this fall I'll have your son in my class."

"Really?" Emily said, smiling.

"Yep. I've seen the class lists for the new school year." Mr. Anderson paused. "I was at the community pool the other day taking a dip, and I saw Trevor swimming. The boy is good, has real potential. That shouldn't surprise me, I suppose, considering what a great swimmer his father was way back when. Mark Maxwell is the reason there are so many swimming trophies on display at the high school."

He chuckled. "Trevor is the spitting image of Mark at the same age, too. Even if I hadn't known all along that Mark is Trevor's father, I sure would figure it out now by comparing the two in my mind."

Emily felt the color drain from her face. "You've always known that Trevor's father is... I didn't realize that it was common knowledge that Mark..." Her voice trailed off, as her mind raced.

"Oh, I don't know that it's common knowledge, as you put it," Mr. Anderson said. "Goodness, Emily, I hope I'm not speaking out of turn here, but you might recall that I was an assistant swim coach in those days. I had to earn extra money to feed our brood and took on that job. I knew you and Mark were going together, and you were always at the swim meets cheering him on. Mark left for Boston after graduation, you have Trevor months later and..."

He shrugged. "Seeing Trevor in the pool the other day was like a flashback. I can remember being sorry at the time that things didn't work out for you and Mark. You two seemed so suited for each other, appeared to be so happy but... Well, you're to be commended on doing a marvelous job of raising your boy alone, Emily. He's a great kid and I'm looking forward to having him in my class."

"Thank you," she mumbled. "I must go. I'm running late. Happy anniversary. Bye."

Emily managed to make it to her car on trembling legs that were threatening to give way beneath her. She slid behind the wheel and leaned her head back, taking several deep breaths.

During all those years that she'd hidden in her house getting fatter by the day, she thought frantically, the humanity beyond her front door had known that Mark Maxwell was Trevor MacAllister's father.

She'd been so dumb, so naive to think that the

people who knew her and Mark wouldn't put two and two together. Heaven only knew how many people were aware of the true facts. There was no doubt in her mind that someone was going to spill the beans to Trevor. Somehow she had to convince Mark that Trevor had to be told by them that Mark was his father before someone else did.

When Mark had suggested that he and Emily go out to dinner since Trevor would be at Jacob's birthday celebration, she had declined the invitation. Saying she had too much to catch up on around the house, she suggested that he come over about seven o'clock, and she'd watch him eat a dish of ice cream.

She really did have a lot to catch up on, Emily thought, as she heard Mark's knock at the door that evening, none of which she wanted to discuss in a restaurant. Good heavens, she wished it was already tomorrow and the heavy-duty discussion was over, the chips having fallen where they may.

She opened the door and produced what she hoped was a passable smile as she greeted Mark. He entered the house, then turned to face her.

"What's wrong?"

"Wrong?" Emily said, raising her eyebrows as she pushed the door closed.

"Hey, this is me...Mark," he said. "I know you very well, remember? That was one of the phoniest smiles I've ever seen."

Emily sighed. "You're right. It was. I have a lot on my mind, Mark. Let's go into the kitchen and I'll serve up the ice cream I promised, then we'll talk. We really do have to talk."

"Forget the ice cream," Mark said, frowning. "What's going on?"

"Okay. Fine. Have a seat."

Mark settled onto the sofa and spread his arms across the top as Emily sat down across the room in an easy chair. She drew a deep breath, let it out slowly, then related what had taken place with Mr. Anderson at the stationery store that afternoon.

"Don't you see, Mark?" she said. "Someone is going to say something to Trevor that will make him take a closer look at you. If he figures out on his own that you're his father the situation will be worse than it already is, which seems impossible but it's true. Trevor must be told the truth now."

"Yes, I understand," Mark said slowly, a frown knitting his brows. "I was so centered on when I wanted to tell Trevor that I'm his father that I didn't think about anything else."

"We've got to sit him down as soon as possible and tell him together. If you do it without me, Mark, Trevor will surely ask you why you didn't marry me and take on the role of his father from the minute he was born."

"And I'd tell him that it wasn't possible because you no longer loved me," Mark said, his voice rising. "Plus the bulletin that I didn't even know he existed until I came back to Ventura for this visit. You don't need to be there when I talk to him, father to son."

"That's not fair," Emily said, her volume matching Mark's. "Then Trevor will come to me demanding to know why I lied to him all of his life."

"Which will be a legitimate question, don't you think?" Mark shifted his arms to prop his elbows on his knees and make a steeple of his fingers. "I'd like the answer to that one myself. Just because you no longer loved me is no excuse for keeping the existence of my son a secret, not letting me know I had a child."

"You don't understand, Mark," Emily said, shaking her head.

"You bet I don't."

"I..." Emily started, then stopped speaking as a chill coursed through her.

This was it, she thought. Truth time. Oh, God, she was so terrified.

"Mark," she said, hearing and hating the quiver in her voice, "there's something you need to know."

"I'm listening," he said, still frowning. "What is it that I need to know?"

"When...when I found out that I was pregnant, my first instinct was to contact you in Boston and tell you. I was so scared, felt so alone and... I must have picked up the receiver to the telephone ten times to call you, but I kept putting it back down."

"Why?" Mark said, nearly shouting. "Why in the hell didn't you tell me you were carrying my baby?"

"Because I loved you too much to do that to you," Emily yelled, then drew a shuddering breath.

"What?" Mark said, his voice a harsh whisper.

"I loved... I loved you so much," Emily said, her eyes filling with unwelcomed tears, "and I needed you here, with me, standing by my side as my husband, the father of our baby. But..." Two tears spilled onto her pale cheeks and she swept them away. "But I knew if I told you I was pregnant, you'd leave Boston and come right back to Ventura to marry me."

"Damn straight I would have."

"Oh, can't you see?" Emily said. "I loved you beyond measure, Mark. If I had told you about the baby, you would have sacrificed everything you'd worked so hard for to be here with us. I couldn't do that to you because I loved you too much to destroy what was then yours, what you'd earned the right to have.

"The letter was a lie. I told my family the same lie so my father wouldn't go to Boston and bring you back here to marry me."

"I don't believe this," Mark said, staring at Emily with an incredulous expression on his face.

"It's true," she said, fresh tears tracking her cheeks. "I kept our baby a secret from you out of love, Mark. Then the years went by and there was never a good time to tell you about Trevor because you were working so hard, making a name for yourself. What I did was done out of the deepest love for you, Mark, I swear it was. That's what we can tell Trevor...together and..."

Mark lunged to his feet, and Emily jerked back in the chair at his sudden motion. He strode across the room, planted his hands on the arms of the chair and leaned down close to her to speak as she stared at him with wide, tear-filled eyes.

"How dare you have made that decision on your own," he said, a muscle ticking in his jaw. "How dare you treat me like a child not capable of making my own choices. How dare you keep my son from me all these years based on what you call love."

"I do love... I *did* love you," Emily said, nearly choking on a sob. "That's why I didn't tell you about our baby, Mark. It was because I loved you so much that I kept silent and—"

Mark straightened and sliced one hand through the air. "Cut. Don't say it again. It's insulting my intelligence, and I don't want to hear it repeated. You loved me? So you wrote me a letter saying you didn't? You kept the existence of my son, *my son,* from me based on the fact that you loved me?

"Emily, you don't know the meaning of love. Love doesn't lie. Love doesn't keep a father from his son.

"No, you don't know how to love, never have and probably never will."

"Mark..." Emily said, crying openly.

"I had the right to know about our baby from the very beginning, before he was even born, damn it," Mark hollered. "I...am...Trevor's...father, Emily."

"But I..."

The front door burst open, and Trevor entered the house. He slammed the door closed behind him and curled his hands into tight fists at his sides. Mark spun around to look at him and Emily got to her feet, brushing past Mark.

"Trevor, what are you doing here?" Emily said. "You're supposed to be at Jacob's."

"Jacob got the stomach flu," Trevor said, his eyes darting back and forth between his mother and Mark. "His mom brought me home and said we'd try again next weekend and... I heard you yelling as I came to the door, Mark. I heard... I heard you say that you're my father."

"Trevor, honey, listen to me," Emily said, taking a step toward him.

"Don't you come near me," Trevor said, his bottom lip trembling as he took a step backward. "You're a liar, Mom. You told me my father was dead. You told me he was an angel in heaven. You told me I should never, ever lie to you about anything and now I find out that you..." He burst into tears. "I hate you, Mother. I hate you, I hate you, I hate you. I could have had a dad...a real dad...just like all the other kids, like Jacob, and...I'll hate you for as long as I live!"

"Trevor, wait a minute," Mark said. "Let's talk this through and..."

"I hate you, too, Mark," Trevor yelled. "You're a liar, too, just like my mom. You came to town and spent time with me, did the swimming junk, and buddied up to me and...

"What were you doing, Mark? Looking me over, sizing me up, deciding if I was good enough for you to claim me as your son? Did I pass your tests, Mark? Well, you don't pass mine. I don't want you for a father and I don't want you for my mother, Mom, not for another second of my life. I hate both of you."

Trevor turned and ran out the door, leaving it open behind him.

"Oh, God, no," Emily said, running to the doorway. "Trevor! Wait! Please, sweetheart. Let me explain why I..."

"Emily," Mark said quietly, "let him go."

She turned and looked at him, a stricken expression on her face.

"How can you say that?" she said. "He's a little boy, a baby, who has just had his world as he's known it his entire life destroyed. He's hurt and angry and confused. We've got to go after him, bring him home, sit him down and—"

"He won't listen," Mark said, dragging one hand through his hair. "Not now. Not yet. Give him some space, some time alone to settle down, think about what he has just learned.

"I think all he heard was me saying that I'm his father. He's going to have questions when he calms down and we'll need to be here with the answers for him."

"But..." Emily said, staring out the open door. "He's out there somewhere crying and..."

"Close the door, Emily. Come on. Leave him alone for now."

"No," she said, shaking her head. "I'm going after him and tell him—"

"Tell him what?" Mark crossed the room and closed the door. "That you lied to me and then lied to him out of love? Whoa. Won't that sound great? That you rewrote that line from the old movie and that love means you get to tell as many lies as you want to? Yeah, right, the kid will really go for that malarkey...about as much as I do, which is not at all."

"Damn you, Mark Maxwell," Emily said, planting her hands on her hips. "You've made up your mind that I never loved you and now you won't budge on the subject. Would you stop and think a minute? About what we had together back then, what we shared? Do you really believe that I was the kind of girl then, or woman now, who would make love with a man she wasn't deeply in love with?

"I won't stand here and remain silent," she raged on, "while you insinuate that I was some cheap little floozy, who... No. I've struggled to get a sense of self, to nurture my self-esteem and, by God, you're not going to destroy it by casting negative shadows over me, attempting to turn me into something that is less than who I am. No, no, no. Have you got that, buster?" Emily drew a much-needed breath. "Goodbye. I am going to go look for our...my son."

"You love me, are in love with me...now?" Mark said, narrowing his eyes.

"What?" Emily said. "Weren't you listening to a word I said? I was trying to get across to you that I loved you so much back when I discovered that I was pregnant that I made the decision..."

"Hold it," Mark interrupted, raising one hand. "You said that you were not the type of girl then, *or woman now,* who would make love with someone unless she was deeply in love with him."

"Don't be absurd," Emily said, with a cluck of disgust. "I did *not* say that. I said..." She stopped speaking, her eyes widened, and a heated flush stained her cheeks. "Oh. Well. I'm upset, terribly, terribly upset, and I didn't intend to say that I... What I mean is...

"Oh, for Pete's sake, what difference does it make? Yes. Yes, Dr. Maxwell, okay fine. Yes. I loved you then and...and...I love you now. I didn't know that I did, but then I did know that I did. Satisfied? It won't mean a tinker's damn to you because you don't believe that I've ever been, nor will ever be, capable of loving anyone."

"Emily..."

"Just...just shut the hell up," she yelled, tears threatening once again. "I'm going out there and find Trevor. But let me tell you something, Mr. Know-it-all. You don't think I ever really loved you? Well, guess what? Our son's name is Trevor *Mark* MacAllister." A sob caught in her throat. "I named my baby after his father. The man I loved with my whole heart. It's a wonder Trevor hasn't zeroed in on the fact that his middle name is Mark, but he will now and... Oh, oh, oh, I'm just done with you, finished. I'm ending this conversation and—"

"Trevor *Mark?*" Mark said, a slow smile creeping onto his lips. "He carries my *first* name because you believed it would have destroyed my future, if he had my *last* name, if I'd come back to Ventura and married you when you found out that you were pregnant?"

"Wow," Emily said. "You finally got it. For a brilliant man, you sure are slow sometimes. Not that you believe that I really loved you. Oh, forget this. I'm going to go look for Trevor and—"

"I believe," Mark said. He closed the distance between them and framed Emily's face in his hands. "I believe that you loved me then and that you love me now. I believe that I was so wrong and said such cruel and hateful things to you that I should, and am, begging you to forgive me.

"And I *know,*" he went on, his voice raspy with

emotion, "that I love you, Emily MacAllister, and that I never stopped loving you."

Emily blinked. "Pardon me?"

"I...love...you," Mark said. "And, oh, man, you love *me.* We can have it all, don't you see? I want to marry you, Emily. I want to be your husband and Trevor's father, be a family, the three of us. Forgive me, please, for the hateful things I said to you. I truly love you and will for the rest of my life. And I love Trevor, too, and will love the brother or sister we'll give him if you're willing. Marry me, Emily. Please. Say that you'll be my wife. Please? Say yes?"

Emily drew a shuddering breath that seemed to come from the very depths of her broken soul. She looked at Mark with tear-filled eyes and spoke one word that held an echo of pain so deep, so chilling, it defied description.

"No."

Ten

Time stopped.

Mark felt as though his world was tilting on its axis, dumping out his life like a scattered jigsaw puzzle. All the pieces were there, but none of them were fitted snugly together the way they belonged in order to complete the desired picture.

"Emily..." he said, reaching out one hand toward her. "Come on. Please. Let's sit down and talk about this and—"

"No," Emily said, shaking her head. "There's nothing to discuss." She drew a shaky breath. "Mark, I made decisions so many years ago that I thought were right for everyone involved. But I was wrong, so terribly wrong.

"Because of those choices my son is suffering the pain of what he sees as a horrendous betrayal by his mother. He now knows that I lied to him and...and he hates me, hates what I've done to him, and he has every right to be hurt and angry.

"It doesn't matter how I might feel about you, or you about me. I have to focus on Trevor, on attempting to somehow repair the damage I've done. I can't think about anything else...only Trevor. I hope, pray, he'll forgive me for the lies, learn to trust me again."

"We'll approach Trevor together, Emily," Mark said. "You're not alone, not anymore. He's angry at me, too, but we'll work it out as a family, put all the pieces of the puzzle together so it's right for everyone. Oh, don't you see? We can have—"

"No," Emily said, her voice rising. "I made the wrong decisions alone. I'll attempt to repair the damage I've done to that little boy alone. I want, I need, to do it this way. If you want to try to mend fences with Trevor you'll have to do it on your own. You and I are *not* together, Mark. I don't have emotional room for an *us*. I'm concentrating on Trevor, nothing more. If this hurts you, I'm sorry, but it's the way it has to be."

"You're doing it again," Mark said, with a flash of anger. "You're making decisions for everyone, especially for me, without my input, my ideas, thoughts, my help. Didn't you learn anything from the last time you did it this way? You were wrong back then, and you're wrong now. Stop and think about what you're doing.

"Damn it, Emily, I'm not a couple of thousand miles away this time, I'm right here, willing, wanting, needing to stand by your side through this. Don't shut me out. Not again. God, Emily, not again."

"I have to do it this way, Mark. I..."

The telephone rang and Emily turned and ran into the kitchen with Mark close behind her. She snatched up the receiver.

"Trevor?" she said.

"No, dear, it's your grandmother," Margaret MacAllister said. "Trevor is here. He's terribly upset, but your grandfather and I have been able to piece together what has happened from the things Trevor is saying.

"He knows that Mark is his father but feels that Mark having kept that truth from him indicates that Mark isn't certain he wants Trevor as his son."

"Oh, Grandma, that's not true," Emily said, blinking away fresh tears.

Margaret sighed. "My darling, Trevor is devastated over the lies you told him about his father being dead. He's a very confused, unhappy little boy."

"I was wrong about so many things, Grandma," Emily said, giving up her battle against the tears. "I'll spend the rest of my life, if that's what it takes, trying to make amends, begging him to forgive me, to trust and believe in me. Love me again."

"Let's just take one step at time," Margaret said gently. "Everyone needs to calm down and sort things through. Trevor is going to spend the night here with us. He's exhausted, isn't thinking clearly right now. I'll call you in the morning."

"Yes. Yes, okay," Emily said, a sob catching in her throat. "Tell Trevor that I love him and... No, he doesn't want to hear that now, won't believe it. Oh, God, what have I done? So many lies."

"That have a way of coming back to haunt a person tenfold, my darling," Margaret said. "Well, what's done is done. Try to get some sleep, Emily. I'm afraid the new day will be filled with difficulties and you'll need to be at your best. Good night."

"Good night, Grandma," Emily said, crying openly. "Take good care of my baby for me."

Emily replaced the receiver, then covered her face with her hands as she gave way to her tears. Mark raised his arms to reach out for her, wanting to hold her close, comfort her, let her know she wasn't alone in her misery, but then dropped his arms heavily to his sides, curling his hands into tight fists.

"Do you...do you want me to leave, Emily?"

Emily nodded, then stumbled to the chair at the table and sank onto it. She folded her arms on the top of the table and buried her face in the crook of one elbow, weeping as though her heart was breaking into a million pieces.

Never in his life, his entire life, Mark thought, staring at Emily, had he felt so impotent, so useless.

His physical size and strength meant nothing. The love he possessed for Emily and their son meant nothing.

The pieces of the puzzle were being scattered by the wind of despair, and he had the sinking, chilling fear that he'd never be able to gather them all together again.

A steady drumming sound reached deep into Emily's mind and pulled her from the darkness. She'd finally fallen into a restless slumber of nightmares. Now she raised her head slowly, foggily deciding that she was in the midst of a strange dream where she was sleeping while hunched over the kitchen table. It was pitch-black except for the tiny lighted numbers on the microwave that declared it to be just after midnight.

The drumming noise continued in a maddening rhythm and Emily got to her feet. She was tired and achy in this dream and she had to quiet the beating tempo so she could rest again.

Hardly realizing she was moving she made her way toward the sound, crossing the dark living room, then opening the front door.

Mark was there.

She could see him clearly in the silvery glow of the moon and stars. Because this was a dream, she didn't have to think, she was allowed only to feel and she lifted her arms to welcome him into her embrace.

Mark stepped forward and drew her close, burying his face in her silky hair as he pushed the door shut with one foot.

"I couldn't stand it another minute," he said, his voice muffled slightly. "I was pacing the floor in my hotel room, kept hearing you crying, so sad, so… I had to come back, Emily, because I love you so much and…"

"Shh," she whispered. "I'm not crying. I'm dreaming. It was a nightmare, I think, but now it's a wonderful dream because you're here, and I love you, and I want to make love with you and… Oh, this is a glorious dream."

Mark raised his head and frowned. "Are you all right? Are you awake? I mean *really* awake, Emily?"

"Tired. I'm very tired. I can't think now because I'm much too tired, but I can feel, and I am, and I want you, Mark."

"No, I won't take advantage of you, Emily. You're not yourself. You've been through so much tonight and… I'll tuck you in bed, then leave. Come on. Let's go down the hall to your room."

Mark encircled Emily's shoulders with one arm and led her to the bedroom, aware that she was weaving on her feet. In her room, he snapped on the lamp on the nightstand, swept back the blankets on the bed, smoothed them, then fluffed the pillow.

When he turned to Emily again she was dropping the last of her clothes to the floor to stand naked before him, the small lamp casting a golden glow over her.

"Ah, Emily, don't," Mark said with a groan, as heated desire rocketed through his body. "You're killing me. You're groggy, not thinking clearly and I won't... No. Get in bed and I'll cover you and... Quickly. Okay? I'm not made of stone. Crawl in here."

"I'm awake now. I really thought I was dreaming when I answered your knock at the door. Mark, I can't dwell anymore tonight on the terrible mess I've made of everything. I'll face it all again in the morning.

"But tonight? I just want to be me, Emily MacAllister, the woman, special, beautiful and yours. I love you, Mark, so much and I refuse to think beyond that fact. Not now. Can't we have this night together, knowing we love each other as we did years ago, never really stopped loving each other? Just one night before the world comes crashing down on me again?"

"I..."

"Please?" she whispered.

It was that one word spoken in such a soft, feminine voice that was a combination of a woman who knew her own mind and a little girl asking for something only he could give that was Mark's undoing.

He closed the distance separating him from Emily, framed her face in his hands and kissed her gently, reverently, pushing into oblivion the knowledge that this might be the last night they would have together.

Emily encircled Mark's neck with her arms and deepened the kiss, savoring the taste, the aroma, the strength and power of Mark, cherishing it all.

Mark broke the kiss only long enough to step back and shed his clothes, then they tumbled onto the bed, reaching for each other eagerly as the heat of desire within them burst into raging flames.

There was no world, no worries or woes, nothing, beyond the two of them and what they were sharing. Their lips met, then tongues met in the sweet darkness of Emily's mouth, as Mark skimmed one hand over her body, igniting a path of fiery need.

He shifted to draw one of her breasts deep into his mouth and Emily whimpered with the want of him. Mark moved to the roundness of her stomach, then lower, kissing, licking, tasting, savoring.

This night, Emily thought hazily, is ours. She was making love with the man she loved so much there weren't words yet invented to describe its intensity. This night was Mark.

Emily, Emily, Emily, Mark's mind hummed. How he loved her. This night was a gift, a chance to use stolen time to put the pieces of the puzzle together and hold fast to the glorious picture they created until the light of dawn blew the jagged pieces apart again.

Emily touched the tip of her tongue to Mark's shoulder, marveling at the salty taste of his moist skin. She splayed one hand on his back and was awed once again by the tight muscles that moved beneath her palm.

What a wondrous man Mark had become, she thought dreamily, and she was his equal, his partner, a woman matching with femininity his incredible masculinity. She was beautiful.

Oh, the heat, she thought. She was consumed by it, was going up in flames of desire so hot she was going to be nothing more than cinders if Mark didn't hurry, quell the fire burning within her. Oh, dear heaven, yes, he had to come to her. Hurry, hurry, Mark, hurry…

"Hurry," Emily said, a sob catching in her throat. "Oh, please, Mark, I can't bear it another second. Hurry, my love. I want you so much."

"And I want you," Mark said, his rational mind buried beneath the heat of passion soaring.

He moved over and into her, filling her, instantly starting a pounding, thundering rhythm that stole the very breath from their bodies. Heat swirled and coiled deep within them, tightening, carrying them up, closer to where they wanted, needed, *had* to travel to…together.

And then they were there.

"Mark!"

It was all, everything, and more than they had ever experienced together before as they were flung into a place of unbelievable splendor. They clung tightly to each other, held fast to the one they loved, wishing with hearts nearly bursting with love never again to let go.

They floated. Unable to speak but mentally calling the name of the other. Down. Slowly. Gently. Returning. Sighing with sated contentment. Etching indelibly in their minds what they had shared.

Mark kissed Emily, then moved off her to settle close to her side. He fumbled for the blankets, drew them over their cooling bodies, then rested his lips on Emily's forehead as she nestled her head on his shoulder.

"I..." Mark started, then paused. "Forget it. I'll never find the words to say how wonderful... No, I can't describe it."

"I know. It was... No, I won't be able to find the words, either."

They were silent for several, reliving-it-all minutes, then Mark suddenly stiffened and shifted up to rest on one forearm, staring at Emily.

"What's wrong?"

"Oh, hell. Oh, man," he said. "Emily, I didn't protect you. I don't believe this. I never made a mistake like that when we were kids and..."

"...and I got pregnant with Trevor despite your precautions."

"There's no excuse for what I just did," Mark went on. "I'm a grown man, for crying out loud. I'm so stupid. I didn't give one thought to—"

"Shh," Emily said, placing her fingertips on Mark's lips. "It's all right. It's the wrong time of the month. Don't worry about it, Mark.'' She smiled. ''Besides, this night is...yes, it's a dream. We'll go back to when I thought I was dreaming when I opened the door and saw you standing there in the glow of the moon and stars. It's all a glorious dream.''

Mark matched her smile. ''You're crazy and I love you, Emily MacAllister.''

''I'm in the midst of a dream of ecstasy and I love *you,* Mark Maxwell,'' Emily said, then her lashes drifted down and she gave way to blissful slumber.

Eleven

They woke at dawn and reached for each other to make slow, sweet love in the shadowy light. Afterward they lay close, not speaking, not wanting to break the loving spell encasing them in a safe and sated cocoon.

"Well," Mark said finally, "when I blow it, I do a great job of it. Not only did I make love to you twice...strike one, strike two...without protecting you, but I also spent the entire night here. The neighbors can have a field day with the fact that my vehicle was in front of your house from dark until dawn. That's strike three. I'm out."

"Not yet," Emily said, snuggling even closer to the warmth of Mark's body. "Soon, but not yet."

She sighed. "I wonder what frame of mind Trevor will be in when he wakes up at my grandparents'."

"Back to reality," Mark said, frowning. "Emily, I know you said that you wanted to talk to Trevor alone, then leave me to speak to him on my own. I really believe it would be better for him, for the three of us, to sit down together and discuss this. I'm guessing that his hurt, anger, at you and me is all intertwined. Why put him through it twice?"

"Well," Emily said slowly, "maybe you're right. Yes, that makes sense. But what if he feels we're ganging up on him, two against one?"

"He's so upset already," Mark said, sifting his fingers through Emily's silky hair, "that we're in a damned-if-we-do, damned-if-we-don't mode anyway. We'll be honest and up-front, answer all of his questions. That's all we can do, Emily."

"He hates me."

"No, Trevor does *not* hate you. That screamer of his was typical adolescent behavior. We hurt him, he hurt us back. Harsh words were the only means of defense he had available."

"How do you know all this? You sound like an expert on the subject."

"I was an I'm-almost-thirteen-years-old boy myself once, remember?" Mark paused. "We're all supposed to be at a birthday shindig at your grandparents' house this afternoon, aren't we?"

Emily wiggled free of Mark's embrace and sat up in the bed. "I forgot all about that. It's at one o'clock. Oh, this is terrible. We can't attend that party with Trevor glowering at us from the opposite side of the room."

"Then I suggest we meet with him well before the scheduled time for the event."

"I'll call my grandparents and tell them we'll be coming over there early to talk to Trevor and..."

"Emily, could we stop a minute here and focus on the fact that we're in love with each other?"

"No."

"Didn't think so," Mark said, then flipped back the blankets on the bed. "I'll get dressed, then go back to my hotel and shower and change. You can call me there and tell me what time to pick you up to go to the summit meeting of the century with our son."

At a little past eleven-thirty, Emily fiddled with the stack of birthday cards in her lap as Mark drove in the light Sunday traffic toward Margaret and Robert MacAllister's house.

"I'm a wreck," she said.

"It shows," Mark said, glancing over at her. "You're going to rub holes in those envelopes if you don't leave them alone. What's in the big container you put on the back seat?"

"A salad for the party," Emily said. "Even if this meeting with Trevor is a disaster and we leave, I wanted to bring what I said I would for the potluck because they're counting on it as part of the meal."

"You always put other people's needs first," Mark said, shaking his head.

"Are you saying that's wrong?" Emily said, a slight edge to her voice.

"Just making an observation. It's definitely a debatable subject, but this is not the day to get into it. Emily, quit messing around with those poor beat-up cards."

"Oh." She plunked the cards next to her on the seat. "I was going round and round about how to sign those dumb things. I'm so mentally worn out that I just gave up and put all three of our names on them."

"As though we're a family. Emily, Mark and Trevor."

"Oh, Mark, don't. I'm hanging on by a thread here. I'm so frightened, so scared to death that I've destroyed the loving relationship I have with Trevor. I'll do anything to make things right between us again."

"Mmmm," Mark said, narrowing his eyes.

He pulled into the driveway at the senior MacAllisters', then turned off the ignition. Emily didn't move, just sat staring at the house, her hands clutched tightly in her lap.

He wanted to gather her into his arms, Mark thought, comfort her, tell her that he was there with her and she wasn't alone. Tell her that everything was going to be just fine. Tell her over and over how much he loved her, would always love her.

But he couldn't do any of those things.

Emily was back to where she had been before the night they'd just shared of incredibly beautiful love-making. The night of the dream. She was centered on Trevor, with no room for anyone else.

"Well, here goes," Emily said, her voice not quite steady as she opened the door to the vehicle.

Margaret and Robert greeted them at the door, saying Trevor was in Robert's study and knew they were coming to talk to him.

"How is he this morning, Grandma?" Emily said, giving her the salad and birthday cards.

"Well, dear," Margaret said, "Trevor is… I wish I could say that he… But the fact is…"

"He's mad as hell," Robert said. "He's hurt, confused and hates the world in general. You two have your work cut out for you. Go on in there. I'm sure he knows you've arrived."

"Bless you both," Margaret said.

"Thank you for everything," Emily said, then drew a deep breath, letting it out in several shaky little puffs of air.

Emily and Mark walked through the house toward Robert's study, Mark finally shoving his hands into his pockets to keep from pulling Emily close to his side.

At the closed door to the study, Emily knocked, waited, heard no reply, then opened the door and entered the cozy room with Mark behind her.

Mark shut the door, then they looked at Trevor,

who was slouched low in one of the high-backed leather chairs by the fireplace, his arms folded tightly over his chest and a stormy expression on his pale face.

His hair was damp from a shower, the cowlick curly on the crown of his head. He was dressed in baggy shorts and a faded T-shirt, chosen from a stash of clothes he kept at his great-grandparents'. His feet were bare.

Emily sat down on a footstool directly in front of Trevor and Mark settled in the other leather chair behind her. Trevor shifted his gaze to his bony knees.

"Trevor? Honey? Mark and I would like to talk to you." Emily hesitated, then continued when Trevor didn't reply. "Oh, Trevor, I'm so sorry I hurt you. That was never my intention, believe me. I want to explain why I made the decisions I did. Will you listen to me? Please?"

Trevor lifted one shoulder in a shrug, still refusing to look at his mother.

"When...when I discovered I was pregnant with you," Emily said, her voice trembling slightly, "Mark had already left for Boston to start college with the scholarship he'd received.

"I loved him so much, so very much, that I didn't tell him about you. If I had, he would have come right back to Ventura to be with us, giving up all his hopes and dreams. I couldn't destroy all he'd worked for, Trevor, I just couldn't. Love is a very powerful emotion, and it gave me the strength and courage to do what I felt was best. I told Mark that I no longer loved him."

"You lied to him," Trevor said, meeting Emily's gaze. "And then you lied to me. You lied and lied."

"Yes, I did," Emily said, lifting her chin. "They were lies born of love, but that doesn't make them right. I was wrong, Trevor, and now I'm paying the pricc for the mistakes I made."

"Why did you tell me my father was dead?"

"Oh, honey. Time went by and there never seemed to be a proper time to tell Mark he had a son. He believed that I didn't love him and was dedicating himself to his career, making a name for himself in his field. You and I were a team, doing so well, making it all work for us that I…I just left things as they were.

"You seemed to accept my lie with no question, and we continued on with our lives. Until Mark returned to Ventura I had no idea that you had yearned for a father all these years, honey. I didn't know, and I'm so sorry."

"Yeah, right," Trevor said, staring at his knees again, his arms still folded tightly over his chest.

"Mark knew you were his son," Emily went on, "the minute he saw you. You look just like he did at the same age. He was very angry at me, Trevor, for keeping you from him. I finally told Mark the truth, said that I had loved him so much back then that I had made the decision to remain silent about you so he could achieve his dreams."

"Mmm," Trevor said.

"Mark wanted to tell you immediately that he was your father, but I convinced him it would be better to establish a relationship with you first. Oh, sweetheart, Mark wasn't...wasn't sizing you up to see if you qualified, or something, to be his son. He wants to be your father. He loves you, just as I do."

"Yeah, right."

"Trevor, listen to me, please," Emily said, feeling the aching sensation of threatening tears in her throat. "You must remember that I was only a few years older than you are now when I made the choices I did. I was so young, didn't have the wisdom that comes with growing, maturing.

"Lies are wrong. *I* was wrong. I should have done things differently, been honest, forthcoming with the truth, just as I've taught you to be. I'm...I'm begging you to forgive me for making the choices I did, for hurting you so much. Please, Trevor."

"I lied to you once last year, remember?" Trevor said. "I said I'd done my math homework and I hadn't. You caught me because you asked to see it before I put it in my backpack.

"You took my bike away from me for a whole week, because I'd lied to you. I said I was sorry, but you didn't care about that. You still wouldn't let me ride my bike.

"You told me never to lie to you again and I

haven't, not once. But you've been lying to me my whole life long, and I really hate you for that. I hate you."

"That's enough, Trevor," Mark said. "I'm not going to sit silently by and allow you to speak to your mother like that. She's talking to you from her heart, and you should respect that, respect *her* for admitting she was wrong, even though at the time that she lied she believed it was the best thing to do."

"Why do you care if I respect my mom, or hate my mom, or whatever, Mark?" Trevor said, volume on high. "She lied to you, too."

"And I now understand why she did it." Mark said quietly. "I'm not certain I deserved that kind of love back then, but your mother gave it to me anyway."

"So you're just going to blow it off?" Trevor yelled. "Say, hey, no problem, Emily, I forgive you for lying to me for a zillion years?"

"It's not a matter of forgiving, Trevor," Mark said, looking directly at his son. "It's accepting the truth that what your mother did was out of the deepest love imaginable. Love for me. Love for you."

"Yeah, right," Trevor said yet again.

"And knock off the 'yeah, right' junk," Mark said. "We've heard enough of that one."

"Trevor," Emily said, "tell me what you want me to do to set things to rights. I want us to be what we were, the team, the loving mother and son. I'll do anything to repair the damage I've done."

A flicker of interest crossed Trevor's face. "Really? What if I said I might go live with Mark since he's going to stay in Ventura?"

A cold chill swept through Emily and tears stung at the back of her eyes.

"Then that's what you'll do," she said, hearing the echo of those tears in her voice, "if it will make you smile, be happy again."

"I might decide to spend some weekends with you. Maybe. I'll have to think about that. I don't know. Maybe I'll live here with my great-grandparents. They're cool. And they never lie to me about anything. Or maybe I'll bunk in with Aunt Jessica and Uncle Daniel. No, he's a cop. He probably has a whole bunch of rules, even more than you do, Mom. I'll let you know what I decide."

Emily straightened on the footstool and stared at Trevor, her mind racing.

Her son, the con artist, was pushing the envelope, she thought. She was like a marionette who had handed over the strings to control her to an immature I'm-almost-thirteen-years-old child, and he was jerking her around emotionally and enjoying every minute of it.

You always put other people's needs first.

The words Mark had spoken to her during the drive over here suddenly screamed for attention in her mind. And they were true, sadly so. Well, not this time. She...was...woman. She had struggled to gain confidence in herself and, by golly, she had it, in spades.

"Fine," she said, getting to her feet. "Keep me posted, let me know where you finally decide to hang your hat in case you get any mail I should forward to you."

"Huh?" Trevor said, his head snapping up to look at her with wide eyes.

"Oh, by the way, Trevor," Emily went on, "there's something you should know. Not only did I love Mark way back when, but I love him now, too. Oh, yes, I love him and he loves me.

"And guess what? I plan to accept Mark's proposal of marriage. Yep, I am. I am going, for what might be the first time in my life, to put my wants, needs, hopes and dreams on the top of the list. It's *my* turn, Trevor, and I'm going to grab hold of the happiness I can have with Mark and never let go."

A grin broke across Mark's face and a warmth suffused him as he listened to the wondrous words and watched Emily's magnificent performance.

"You're going to marry Mark? You're going to have a gushy, mushy wedding and everything? You're going to live in the same house together? But what about me?"

"We certainly hope you'll drop by as often as you can," Emily said, studying the nails on one of her hands.

"But I'm your son," Trevor said, jumping to his feet. "You're my mom and Mark's my dad and…"

"Ah, but don't forget," Emily said, raising one finger. "I'm the mother who lied to you. Lies of love, but still lies. You hate me, remember? Oh, you'll have to take Mark's name off your list of possible candidates for who you might choose to live with, because he'll be living with me. And the baby brother or sister we hope to be blessed with in the future."

She was incredible, this woman he loved, Mark thought. Absolutely dynamite.

"But, Mom?" Trevor said, his voice quivering. "I don't really hate you. I mean, yeah, I was mad and my stomach hurt, but I did listen to what you told me about the lies of love and…and everything.

"You messed up a bunch of stuff, but you didn't mean to. When I told you I did my homework but I didn't, that was a real lie. Your lies were different because you thought it was the only way to love me and Mark the best you could and…

"Mom?" he said, tears filling his eyes. "I'm sorry I was so mean and said that I… Please? I want to come home. You'll be my mom, and Mark will be my dad, and I'll be your kid and we'll be a family. A family, Mom. I love you, I swear I do and… Mommy? Please?"

Emily opened her arms and Trevor hurled himself into her embrace, nearly knocking her over. She held him tight, allowing tears to spill onto her cheeks, feeling the hitch in Trevor's breathing that said that he was crying, too.

"I love you so much, Trevor," Emily whispered.

"I love you, too, Mom. Awesomely much."

Mark got to his feet. "Am I allowed to take part in this group hug?"

"Yes," Emily and Trevor said in unison.

Mark wrapped his arms around his wife-to-be and his son, his own eyes misting with tears.

"A family," he said, his voice husky with emotion. "We're a little late getting started, but now we're all together, home, where we belong."

"The Maxwell family," Emily said, loving shining in her tear-filled eyes. "At long last."

"Cool," Trevor said. "Way cool."

Epilogue

The following two months seemed to fly by so fast that Emily felt as though she had just torn a page off the daily calendar when it was time to remove another.

Mark and Trevor flew to Boston to pack and ship Mark's belongings and sublease his apartment. While there, Mark took Trevor on a tour of the city, then on to New York to see the sights. While in the city, Mark met with a literary agent and presented his proposal for the book he hoped to write, which was received with a great deal of enthusiasm.

Emily was busy planning the wedding with her mother and grandmother. It was to be a family-only affair with a reception at Jillian and Forrest's home.

Emily selected a lovely pale-blue suit as her bridal outfit, with matching shirts for Mark and Trevor that they would wear with dark suits. Jessica was to be the matron of honor and Trevor was chosen to be Mark's best man.

As they had done for Jessica and Daniel, Jillian and Forrest and Margaret and Robert offered a wedding gift of the couple's choice of a lot owned by Malone Construction on which to build their home. And as he had done for Jessica and Daniel, Ryan Sharpe, who was also a cousin to Emily and the others, offered to draw up the plans for the house as his present to the bride and groom.

Emily and Mark would have a short honeymoon trip up the coast to San Francisco and return on Labor Day evening so they would be home in time to see Trevor off on the first day of school.

To add to the building excitement, a telephone call came from the Island of Wilshire with the wonderful news that both Maggie and Alice were pregnant. Jessica said it sounded like the perfect time to make the announcement that she and Daniel were also expecting a baby. Forrest MacAllister made plans to put the long-standing tradition of the MacAllister baby bet into operation.

On the day before the wedding, Emily closed the office in the early afternoon and arrived home to find Mark and Ryan at the kitchen table, which was covered in large sheets of paper.

"Hello, love," Mark said, rising to give Emily a searing kiss.

"Hi," Emily said, then staggered slightly when Mark released her. "Is Trevor still swimming over at the community center?"

Mark laughed. "Yep. Our boy will be growing fins at the rate he's going."

"What?" Emily asked. "Oh. Fins. Yes. Like a fish. Got it."

"Is something wrong?" Mark said.

"Bride jitters," Ryan said, getting to his feet. "All the MacAllister gals get nuts the day before the wedding. It's fascinating to watch...from a distance. Emily, before you fall apart completely, come look at the last of the changes I've made to your house plans. Mark says they're right on the money."

Emily moved closer to gaze at the complicated drawing.

"Fine. Great," she said, nodding. "I can't understand those things. I'll take your word for it. We do thank you for your lovely gift, Ryan."

Ryan kissed her on the forehead. "You've thanked me fourteen times, cousin. Just be happy and when this house is built, turn it into a home filled with love and laughter." He paused. "I...I envy you, both of you, for what you have together."

"Oh, Ryan," Emily said, giving him a hug, then smiling up at him, "your soul mate is out there somewhere. It's just a matter of being patient and waiting until your paths cross. Don't give up on finding that very special woman who will be your partner for life."

"It's a nice thought," Ryan said, "that she's out there just waiting for me to find her but..." He shook his head. "I guess maybe I don't quite believe that will ever happen. Hey, ignore me. No gloomy stuff the day before the big event." He rolled up the papers. "I'll see you tomorrow at the wedding."

"Okay," Emily said.

"Thanks again, Ryan," Mark said.

When Ryan had left the house, Emily frowned as she stared at the door he closed behind him.

"Ryan is so alone. I wish he was as happy as we are, Mark. He has struggled for so many years to accept his half-American and half-Korean heritage, and he seems so lost, and—"

"Whoa," Mark said, encircling her waist with his arms. "I'd like to see a real smile on Ryan's face, too, but this isn't the time to address that dilemma. I want to know what's wrong. I have a feeling there's more going on with you than bride jitters. Talk to me."

"Well, I... You see, I... What I'm trying to say is, Mark... But I don't know how to tell you that...I..."

"Emily, what is it?" Mark shifted his hands to her shoulders. "You haven't changed your mind about marrying me, have you?"

"No," she said, "but you might change your mind about marrying me, because I'm not just a *me*

I'm a *we* and I don't know if you want to start out with a *we* because it was supposed to be later, in the future, and..."

"Emily! What are you talking about?"

"I'm pregnant," she said, then burst into tears.

Mark opened his mouth, closed it, shook his head slightly, then tried again.

"You're...carrying my...our baby?"

"Yes," she said, then sniffled.

"I didn't protect you those two times we made love and... You're pregnant?"

"Would you quit that? It isn't going to go away if you keep saying it over and over again. It isn't going to go away at all. I'm two months pregnant, and—"

"And," Mark said, framing her face in his hands and smiling at her with tears shimmering in his eyes, "this is the most incredibly fantastic, wondrous wedding present you could have given me."

"Really?"

"Oh, yes, really."

"You're going to watch me get fatter and fatter before I had a chance to finish getting thinner and thinner," Emily wailed. "But I want this baby so much, and I love you so much, and I—"

Mark silenced her babble with a kiss that stole the very breath from her body just as Trevor came in the front door.

"Oh, geez," Trevor said, "you guys are hugging

and kissing and crying, and the wedding isn't even until tomorrow."

Mark broke the kiss and nestled Emily close to his side, turning them both to look at their son.

"Tomorrow," Mark said, smiling, "is the beginning of this family's forever. Come on over here and join us, because your mother and I have something very special to share with you...big brother."

* * * * *

Be sure to watch for
Ryan's story, coming to
Silhouette Special Edition
this December.
And now for a sneak preview,
please turn the page.

One

"I'm sorry to have..." Carolyn St. John started, then stopped as she swept her gaze over the man standing in front of the desk. Mr. Ryan Sharpe of MacAllister Architects was, without a doubt, one of the most handsome, well-built men she had ever seen. He was, she guessed, about six feet tall, had dark brown, wavy hair, tawny skin and drop-dead gorgeous, extremely dark, almond-shaped eyes.

Clearing her throat, she tried again. "I'm Carolyn St. John, assistant for Hands Across the Sea International Adoptions. The others are waiting for us in the conference room to review the plans you're presenting for the new building. Were you offered something to drink?"

Ryan pulled his gaze from the photographs on the wall and turned to look at Carolyn St. John. Pretty woman, he thought immediately. Really lovely. Carolyn St. John was about five-foot-six, slender, had curly dark hair that sort of fluffed around her face and fell to just below her ears and the bluest eyes he'd ever seen.

But he'd been so engrossed in looking at the pictures on the wall that he hadn't heard one word she had been saying beyond asking if he'd been offered refreshments.

"Yes, thank you, but I don't care for anything to drink," he said, smiling slightly. He switched his gaze back to the wall of pictures. "I assume these are children from overseas that have been adopted by their new American parents."

Carolyn nodded, closing the distance between them. "I'm in charge of Asian adoptions. Those are photographs of children from various Asian countries who I was involved in placing here in the States with couples and single people, as well." She smiled. "It's my gallery of happiness and dreams come true."

"Happiness and dreams come true," Ryan said quietly, but with a slight edge to his voice, "for the parents. I qualify to have my picture at six months old on a wall like that because my parents adopted me from Korea." Ryan paused and looked at Carolyn St. John again, a deep frown on his face.

"I know you believe you're performing a service

here by providing these children with a chance at a life far better than what they would have had in an orphanage,'' he went on, ''and you are, to a point. But have you ever considered the far-reaching ramifications of placing foreign children with American parents? Have you thought what it's like for those kids when they realize they're different? Do you ever think about that when you're handing out cute little babies from overseas?''

How dare he pass negative judgment on her and the agency! He accused her of not knowing what it was like to be different. Oh, ha, a lot he knew. She had first-hand knowledge of that loner status.

But no matter what difficulties he might have had while growing up, and no matter what problems the precious children she helped place with parents in his country might encounter, they were far better off here than lost in the shuffle in overcrowded orphanages.

''First of all, Mr. Sharpe,'' Carolyn said, with a flash of anger, ''we don't *hand out* those children to just anyone. You're obviously only part Korean, but...'' She planted her hands on her hips. ''I'm sorry if you had difficulties with your mixed heritage while growing up, but... No, I'm not going to justify what I...what we do here to someone who has a chip on his shoulder as wide as Toledo.''

Man, Ryan thought, who had put a rotten nickel in him, causing him to mouth-off like that? Those photographs he'd been staring at had caused painful memories to rise up from the dusty corner of his mind. But that was no excuse for what he had just done, said. Not only had he represented MacAllister Architects very poorly, he had also alienated a very attractive woman. A woman who, when angry, had eyes like incredible blue laser beams and a pretty flush on her cheeks.

He had to apologize to Carolyn St. John, make amends…right now.

"Carolyn," Ryan said finally. "Look, I'm sorry about what I said. I was way out of line, and I apologize for my outburst. It's just that I… No, there's no excuse for my behavior. I'd like to make amends. After the meeting, would you have lunch with me?"

Carolyn stared at him.

"Lunch?" he repeated, producing his best one-hundred watt smile. "Please, Carolyn?"

"I bet you're accustomed to getting just about anything you want with that smile. Well, chalk this up to a new experience for you. Have lunch? With you? Do let me know if there's any part of this reply to your request that you don't understand, but my answer is really quite simple. No."

* * * * *

COMING NEXT MONTH

#1465 TAMING THE OUTLAW—Cindy Gerard

After six years, sexy Cutter Reno was back in town and wreaking havoc on Peg Lathrop's emotions. Peg still yearned passionately for Cutter—and he wanted to pick up where they had left off. But would he still want her once he learned her precious secret?

#1466 CINDERELLA'S CONVENIENT HUSBAND—Katherine Garbera

Dynasties: The Connellys

Lynn McCoy would do anything to keep the ranch that had been in her family for generations—even marry wealthy Seth Connelly. And when she fell in love with him, Lynn needed to convince her handsome husband they could have their very own happily-ever-after.

#1467 THE SEAL's SURPRISE BABY—Amy J. Fetzer

A trip home turned Jack Singer's life upside down because he learned that beautiful Melanie Patterson, with whom he'd spent one unforgettable night, had secretly borne him a daughter. The honor-bound Navy SEAL proposed a marriage of convenience. But Melanie refused, saying she didn't want him to feel obligated to her. Could Jack persuade her he wanted to be a *real* father…and husband?

#1468 THE ROYAL TREATMENT—Maureen Child

Crown and Glory

Determined to get an interview with the royal family, anchorwoman Jade Erickson went to the palace—and found herself trapped in an elevator in the arms of the handsomest man she'd ever seen. Jeremy Wainwright made her heart beat faster, and he was equally attracted to her, but would the flame of their unexpected passion continue to burn red-hot?

#1469 HEARTS ARE WILD—Laura Wright

Maggie Connor got more than she'd bargained for when she vowed to find the perfect woman for her very attractive male roommate. Nick Kaplan was turning out to be everything *she'd* ever wanted in a man, and she was soon yearning to keep him for herself!

#1470 SECRETS, LIES…AND PASSION—Linda Conrad

An old flame roared back to life when FBI agent Reid Sorrels returned to his hometown to track a suspect. His former fiancée, Jill Bennett, was as lovely as ever, and the electricity between them was undeniable. But they both had secrets….

SDCNM0902